Vicious Heart

By Candi Scott

To Anna, with all my heart. For Daniel, because love transcends.

CONTENTS

One

RILEY

His body vibrated with tension, pushing slightly against me, as if I gave him an inch he'd take it all the way to Preacher and knock him right in his teeth. His hands formed fists, his muscles grew impossibly tighter; he practically pulsed with violence.

I hugged him tighter, nuzzling my face just under his neck. The scent of him reminded me of what we'd done, of sex and all the rest. But more, his heart thundered against my cheek. This was scarier than racing through the desert, chased by rednecks. If he acted on the emotion running through him, he could lose so much...*we* could.

I wouldn't be the cause of it. The fear wound tighter. I'd lost so much, and my relationship with Cam was the first thing to make me happy in too long to remember. I'd do anything to keep that feeling, to keep him safe.

"Please." I whispered, barely audible over the music and conversation.

He glanced down, blue eyes bright with an electric energy that threatened to burn it all down around us. It excited me almost as much as it scared me.

"Cam..."

His hands relaxed and his arms wrapped around me, pulling me close and holding me tight, lips seeking mine. The kiss wasn't soft or comforting, it was searing and arousing. Stoking an entirely different fiery sensation. Especially considering that the entire clubhouse saw it, even the patch bunnies.

But it wasn't them he wanted to see. That show was for Preacher, staking his claim, reminding the other man the only thing standing between the two of them was me.

I shivered.

When he pulled free, his hand slid to my ass and gripped it tightly, squeezing enough that I gasped. The look he shot over my shoulder was full of possessive warning. I didn't bother turning around to see Preacher's reaction.

"Come on." His hand moved to my hip as he walked me toward the back door, where Merc stood with it propped open.

"You alright?" Cam turned to me as the door shut behind him, leaving the three of us walking around to where the bikes were parked.

"Yeah." Not a lie; I was a little shaken but otherwise fine. "Today was...stressful."

Cam's eyebrows rose in a *yeah-right* look as he threw a leg over his bike and handed me the helmet. "What did Preach say?"

"Nothing really. I just don't like him," I mumbled, strapping the helmet on.

He wasn't buying it. Stopping short of cranking the bike, he shot me a no bullshit glare. We weren't going anywhere until I told him.

"He asked about the lawyer—Archer shit. Offered to have the club buy the house."

Cam frowned, but he gestured for me to hop on and glanced to Merc, who grunted and climbed onto his bike. "Don't tell him shit, okay?"

It was my turn to make a *yeah right* face as I hopped on. "I got it, trust me." I settled my feet on the pegs and wrapped my arms around his middle. This was the part that was too easy to get used to. The loud reverberation in my chest as he cranked the bike was like a weird calling. Something that would forever be Cam's. No matter how far apart we were, that sound would bring up images of him, feelings of being with him.

Something to hold on to when I couldn't cling to him.

I didn't know where we were going, didn't need to. Like this, I felt safe. Something about Cam and Merc together was sort of invincible, even after we'd been chased through the desert earlier that day. The bond between them was obvious and showed as they rode. Both Harleys staggered in the right lane, Merc always slightly ahead of us, as if the only person he trusted behind him was Cam.

Probably was.

They changed lanes and passed cars in tandem, as if they were following an invisible line in the pavement that only they could see. It made the ride soothing, a balm on the rawness of the day. As I relaxed, I leaned heavier on Cam.

He slipped a hand over mine at his stomach, rubbing my knuckles with his thumb.

The Black Cat sat on the outskirts of Vegas. The dark building's red, neon lady perched on the roof alternated stroking the silhouette of a black cat and herself as she flashed from one scene to another. The back lot was filled with cars, though Merc drove by them and parked by a sleek, black Jag off to the side with a large gray SUV.

As I climbed from the motorcycle and took off the helmet, I was immediately self-conscious. The women in there weren't something I could compete against, not for any man's attention much less Cam's.

Cam, currently interpreting my hesitation, grabbed me by the waist, smacked me on the ass, and dropped a kiss to my lips. "Whatever you're telling yourself, you're wrong."

I'd been in bed with him, watched the way his face changed when he touched me. He was mine. He chuckled when I gave him a wry grin. "Maybe we could put you to work," he teased with a wink and nodded toward the building.

When I cut him a scathing look, Merc piped up with an uncharacteristic good humor. "You're one of us now. Time to earn your keep."

They both fought for serious faces, and I couldn't help but snort a laugh. Away from the clubhouse, they were both so very different, relaxed. They were happy.

"I have zero rhythm. You won't make much off me."

"You've got all the moves I need." Cam stopped walking long enough to kiss me long and slow, then broke with a grin.

Everything in me turned hot and flashed straight to arousal. No, I wasn't the least bit concerned about the women in that club. Not when he did things like that.

"Cut it out, the Soletsky's charge for that shit." But Merc was still grinning.

Cam released me and went in first, past the lone security guard at the back door. That door man stuck a big, beefy arm out to stop me from entering. "Gentlemen only."

"She's with me." Merc pushed his arm out of the way, leading me in before Cam could say anything.

The guard blinked, as if seeing Merc for the first time, then climbed back on his stool, in an unconcerned way that said he knew him well.

"My boy's got sway." Cam smirked.

Merc's dry response was swallowed up by the swell of music.

I'd never been in a strip club before but hadn't expected it to be this loud. Or this clean. The cool air smelled of expensive liquor and vanilla. The scent evoked a sensual image in my head. As did all the dark wood-grain textures and black painted walls.

If it were possible for the inside of a building to ooze sex, this one did.

Near the bar, Merc turned off and ducked down a dark hallway. We didn't follow, instead Cam took my hand and led me around to the bar. At first, I tried not to look, focusing on the bottles lined neatly and shelf in front of the mirrored barback. But then a tall, leggy dancer on a side stage caught my attention. She was topless, her dark nipples sparkled under the flashing lights. She moved like liquid sex, wrapping around the pole and back off again.

Not the ass shaking, stage humping I'd expected. This was a show, each fluid movement of her body meant to draw the eye, intended to arouse. The men tossing money at her were enchanted. Hell, I was too.

"You like her?" Cam whispered against my ear before nipping the lobe.

She was curvy, with dimples in the small of her back. Her thick curtain of dark hair shone and shimmered under the disco ball above the stage. Her full lips twisted into a come-hither smile as she hit her knees and spread her thighs to let a man shove a wad of bills in the garter on her thigh. There was something sexy in the way she chased his touch with her hands, pushing them away and taking his money before spinning back on her pole.

She had my full attention. Or maybe Cam did.

My skin was warm and I shivered when he bit my ear again, with a little more force this time. Cam's presence made everything... *more*. More Demanding. More heated. More sexual.

"Maybe." I definitely liked the feel of his hand on my inner thigh when I slid onto the barstool and the heat as he nuzzled my neck.

The dancer spun around and arched her back, so the men between me and the stage had an unobstructed view of her full ass. When she shook it a little, they all scrambled closer, as if she were moving just for them.

If I'd had a few dollars, I'd have slid them into her thong myself.

When I glanced over to say as much to Cam, he wasn't watching her—he watched me. His eyes narrowed, his nostrils flared a little, like we'd not just had sex a few hours before.

The cool club was suddenly very hot. Were we not in public, the way he was looking at me, I'd have climbed all over him right then. Instead, I blushed and dropped my gaze.

He continued to stroke my thigh, even as he gave the bartender our drink order, his fingers creeping closer to the heat between my legs with each stroke. Then he flicked the tips of his fingers across the hem that covered my pussy. I snapped my legs shut and he chuckled, nipping again at the side of my neck.

Trying to ignore his other hand, that was sneaking up my side, under my shirt, I checked out the main stage. It was larger than any of the others, positioned below the DJ booth, with a mirrored floor that gave spectators a full view of each dancer. My eyes were drawn there, to the flashing lights and the voluptuous woman who teasingly pulled off the skintight dress to the beat of the music.

I was aroused, more from Cam's teasing touches, than anything else. But I didn't look away. My nipples strained against my bra.

Women weren't my thing, but the way she moved was so sensual it triggered illicit fantasies, things I wanted from Cam but couldn't put into words. Cam's fingers stroked over my thighs again and up my ribs, while she swayed and moved. Her body was practically made to evoke the most tempting images.

Cam pulled his hand from my side and handed me a shot of tequila. I watched him grab his beer bottle and take a long pull, the liquid leaving his lips shining, making me want to lick them... and then lick other things.

I closed my eyes against the thought before leaning back against him and opening them to take my shot. On the stage, the woman undulated, drawing every eye close by. I couldn't even make out what the DJ said to egg her on. It didn't matter; all that mattered was watching her was like watching a woman writhe on the bed, begging for more. Even in a crowd of people it was seductively intimate.

Cam leaned close, his body tight against my side, his hand higher between my thighs now, applying gentle pressure. But still, I didn't open them for him. If I did, we'd get thrown out. Occasionally he'd flick his eyes to the dancer, now nude, then back to me, gauging my reaction.

When I licked his lips, I could see him groan, though wished I could have heard it over the music.

He dropped his head to my temple, speaking directly into my ear, his voice thick and husky. "Watching you is probably the hottest thing I've ever seen. I can't wait until I get you home and show you exactly what you make me think about."

Heat fanned out across my chest, traveling fast up my neck to my cheeks.

"Never thought I'd see you bring a woman in here." A slightly accented male voice called over the music, broke whatever sexual spell the place wove over me. "Maybe taking them out, but never in."

I motioned for another shot and the bartender was there instantly. My new shot came so fast I knew the man Cam turned to was important. I downed the shot, the sharp liquid doing little to quell my arousal or my curiosity.

The man who approached was taller than Cam but lean, with a narrow waist and broad shoulders. He was young, too young to run a place like this. Too pretty, too.

He pulled Cam into a back slapping bro hug. Cam's jeans and leather vest contrasted against the other man's black dress slacks and dark t-shirt. The expensive kind that would never dare to attract the little balls of worn fabric in the wash.

"Send a few bottles up to the VIP lounge," he called to the bartender, then turned to me with a smile that was as disarming as it was charming. "Ky Soletsky, the best looking and nicest Soletsky in residence."

Behind him was another man, older but no less attractive and dressed very similarly. His mouth quirked like he might argue, but he was too amused. His high, sharp cheekbones cut a dangerous picture through his five o'clock shadow, so when he smiled it was almost wolfish. He looked far more dangerous than his counterpart, like each breath he took hinted at impending violence.

I didn't have a chance for trepidation to settle in. Because Cam's face lit with genuine pleasure and surprise when he saw the other man. "Val. Good to see you, brother. I was expecting Symon."

"For you, I'm here." His accent was heavier and oddly appealing.

Cam pulled me off the stool and to his side. "Valentyn, this is Riley Bowman."

The harder, edgier Soletsky, seemed to let the weight of my last name settle on him before giving me a genuine smile. "Welcome to The Black Cat. Don't let my nephew deceive you. He's not the best looking."

Ky was cute, seriously. But I had to agree with Val.

Jealousy flashed briefly on Cam's face as Val and I sized each other up. He narrowed his eyes and tucked me against him. His reaction shouldn't be so hot, and yet I licked my lips.

Val laughed, took my hand and brushed a chaste kiss over my knuckles before releasing me and waving for us to follow him. He paused briefly at the main stage, exchanging a glance with the curvy dancer as she bent to pick up her dress. Then she looked past him, smiled at me, and blew me a kiss.

I blushed and looked away, walking side by side with Cam. His free hand on the small of my back was warm and possessive as he directed me up a set of winding stairs behind Val. At the top, I turned to see Merc behind Cam, scanning the club. Out in public, away from the clubhouse, Merc seemed tense, always looking out for trouble—and always right behind him.

Compared to the ride over here, everything about this encounter shouted that it wasn't personal, no matter how pleasantly we were greeted.

Two

CAM

Damn. She looked good. Like she belonged here...to me. The wounded bird persona she'd clung to was long gone. Before me was a confident, sexy woman. I should be proud. And I was, except all I could think about was how I wanted to bite my way up her legs. Start at the top of each boot and go all the way to the frayed edges of her shorts.

But I couldn't, not here. Instead, I watched her as Ky ushered in several dancers, each one more beautiful than the next. None of them holding a candle to Riley.

Somewhere, lust had begun to blur with obsession. It wasn't about keeping her safe anymore. It was about keeping her here with me for as long as I could have her. Because without her—I didn't want to contemplate that tailspin.

A few of the girls flirted with Ky and Merc, two went to the tiny stage, and one perched on Merc's lap. He'd already turned the money over. That business was handled. Nothing we'd speak about up here needed to be kept quiet.

Not that I wanted to talk about the fight or anything else. Beside me, Riley watched the dancers on the tiny stage, her eyes heavy. I hadn't expected her to enjoy herself quite so much. Now that I'd seen it, I wanted to take her home and fuck her until neither of us could move.

Jesus.

"We start with eight fighters, trim it to four, then two for the finale?" Val swirled a dark liquid in his glass. "Who are the Kings putting in the ring?"

"Jester and his little brother." I doubted Val would be surprised by the former, but he gave a short bark of laughter when I mentioned the younger.

"He any good?" But his pleasure showed in the way he leaned back, looking smug.

The Vaughn brothers were notoriously scrappy. They had an uncle make it pretty far in the MMA circuit, and he had trained them both.

Merc, unbothered by the half-naked woman stroking his hair and his ego, snorted. "The kid is something else. Nineteen, wiry, but dangerous. Remind you of anyone?" He flicked a glance to Ky—who would also be fighting.

"I haven't been wiry since high school." The younger Ukrainian wasn't wrong, but he wasn't bulky like his uncle's bodyguard either.

Val grinned. "I've two more I'm entering. A couple of townies also ponied up the cash."

Something skittered across my skin, this weird prickling of unease, because I knew before he said it at least one would be Wanda's. I reached for the back of my neck, scratched that uncomfortable itch.

"The holy trinity of white trash," Val rolled his eyes and his left shoulder simultaneously. "I figured the Kings wouldn't mind mopping the mat with them."

We wouldn't.

"All three will be out first round," Merc added.

"Shall it be so." Val nodded upward, then touched his glass to Merc's bottle.

Riley had cocked her head and followed the conversation with curious interest. She leaned into me. "The guys who chased us will be at the fight?"

"Probably," I answered and brushed my lips across her hair. Having her close enough to touch was something I was getting all too accustomed to. I reached for her knee and stroked the soft skin that ran up toward her thigh.

Her eyes went big, uncertain.

It was Val's turn to be interested. "Something I should be concerned about?"

"Nah," Merc cut me a glance, telling me I needed to shorten Riley's leash. "The normal game Wanda's always tried to run. Probably the same reason she's putting her boys in the fight."

Val looked to me for confirmation, and I gave it to him. "A Dry Valley Dust Up earlier; we took care of it."

I pulled my hand from Riley's leg, ignoring her look of confusion. The rest of the conversation I left to Merc. The Ukrainians were his show. Ky and Val were both appeased with my answer, their attention turned to the set up for the fight. Shit I didn't care about.

Riley shouldn't have said anything. For the first time since I met her, I was going to have to put her in her place. Merc would expect it, the table would.

Fuck.

"Come here." I stood, took her by the hand, and pulled her behind me toward the bathroom. Behind us, Ky shouted to wait until we got home. I ignored him.

In the single occupancy VIP bathroom, I locked the door behind us. The music was muted, but the deep bass still vibrated through the walls.

"What is going on?" Her hazel eyes were wide and startled.

"You can't say shit like that when we are here. Alright?" I barked, harsher than I should have. But if the shit with Preacher got back to any of the club, if Ky said something to anyone else? The blowback would be on me—or worse, on her.

"Fine. Got it." But she'd flinched and turned away from me, hurt.

I grabbed her arm before she could storm out of the bathroom. The money I'd had today had belonged to the Soletskys, if they'd known someone tried to take it from me—it would fuck up too much shit. But I couldn't tell her that. "This is important, Riley. Shit that happens to the MC, stays there. Got it? But what happened today could have fucked up our business here with the Solestkys. You've got to be smarter."

"So, I'm stupid?" She narrowed her eyes and tried to pull away from me. When I didn't let go, she yanked, her cheeks reddening. "Maybe if you actually told me something, I wouldn't mess up."

I clutched tighter, drug her against my chest even as she wriggled. "I tell you what I can."

"You're hurting me." Her eyes welled with tears and my chest twisted tight, painful.

"Think Preacher won't hurt you worse?" And that's what scared me. She could get pissed, throw a fit, but if she was safe, I was okay with that. Preacher was already searching for ways to make the bad shit

Riley's fault. I needed her to understand that, to know I didn't keep secrets because I wanted to. I did it to keep her safe.

If he hurt her...

She closed her eyes. "*Let. Me. Go.*" The anger resonated off her. God, she was beautiful.

I did, and she spun away, storming out of the bathroom. I'd expected her to stomp all the way out, back down to the bar, maybe even outside.

But she surprised me, stopping at the stage, talking directly to the stacked dancer she'd watched so closely downstairs. The dancer smiled, and I stayed in the doorway between the hall and the VIP room, watching.

I couldn't fucking look away.

The dancer ran her fingers through Riley's hair. The touch was very obviously flirty, but Riley didn't knock it away. I tempered the momentary jealousy when Riley glanced back at me, sneered, and took the dancer's hand.

Jesus Christ. I pulled a cigarette from my vest pocket, lit it, and took a long drag. My irritation twisted, spinning around as the dancer, coated in glitter and little else, led Riley to an empty part of the couch near the stage. Anticipation clawed its way up my throat and suddenly the cigarette wasn't doing it for me.

Riley was, though, as she sat watching me with narrowed, angry eyes. The little bitch knew exactly what she was doing to me. And God, I wanted all of it.

The woman straddled her, moving sensuously on her lap, rolling her body in ways that were meant to simulate what I wanted them to do to each other. Fuck if it didn't turn me sideways.

I itched for a joint, hell anything to cool the heat that snaked up my chest and around my neck. The air grew thick, hard for me to breathe, but hell, I couldn't look away. I crushed the cigarette out in the tall ashtray by the door.

The dancer spun on her lap, took Riley's hands, and brought them to her own bare breasts. There, she encouraged Riley to touch, to kneel, to stroke. My cock went rock hard.

Not because my girl was touching another woman, but because Riley was aroused. I could see it in the flare of her nostrils, the part in her lips, the way her own hips shifted on the seat.

Then the dancer turned her head, leaning back, and kissed her. I watched, trapped in every man's wet dream. I was transfixed in the soft way their lips danced on each other, how Riley suckled the other woman's tongue into her mouth, then looked right at me.

I pulled a hundred-dollar bill from my pocket, stalked across the room, and tucked it none too gently into the dancer's tiny red thong.

"I'm cutting in." I took her hand and pulled her off Riley's lap.

"Too bad." She pouted, pulled her hand free, and sashayed back to the stage.

Riley glared at me.

"Time to go."

She stopped just shy of wriggling from my grasp when I pulled her against my chest and she felt why we were leaving.

Her lips formed the sexiest, wettest 'O' of surprised I'd ever seen. "I see."

Three

Riley

I was angry. My arm still stung from where he'd clutched it so tight. I'd been embarrassed I'd caused him problems and that I was being reprimanded. But the callous way he'd spoken to me, looked at me, hadn't scared me.

He'd pissed me off. Even more his thinking he could bully me into submission.

I knew better than to start a fight right in front of everyone. I'd gotten that message loud and clear.

This one was coming in crystalline. The wildness in his eyes, the feel of his arousal against my stomach, the way his body stopped short of trembling. I hadn't just made him jealous; I'd turned him on a ridiculous degree.

And I liked it.

He moved fast, tucking me against him and tossing a hand signal in the air to Merc. A quick, we've got to go. Judging by Val Soletsky's boisterous, knowing laugh—they all knew why.

"You make quite a show, darlin'," he whispered in the brief pause as the DJ switched songs.

The club flashed by after that, a blur of flashing lights and body parts. He didn't run, but Cam threaded through the crowd like his boots were on fire. Anticipation licked up from my middle. The dancer had been sexy; even I couldn't deny that.

But the way Cam had watched me, the reaction the lap dance evoked in him—was so much more.

The evening air was cool, the sun was an afterthought on the horizon, the sky more purple than blue or pink. Cam stopped on the broken pavement, glanced to his left and then to his right before pulling me to the right around the side of the building.

A smaller building butted up to the side, window-less and barely noticeable, painted the same color as the desert beyond. Designed to be nondescript in the ways of onsite storage. He spun, pushing me against the building.

I had a second to gasp before his mouth crushed down on mine. His hands gripped my hips, lifting until my legs wrapped around his waist. His kiss took no prisoners, ripped me open raw, and took everything.

Whatever anger I'd had and the embarrassment that still tumbled around in my brain were sucked up in a vortex of sensation.

He turned me inside out.

I kissed him back, one hand around the side of his neck, the other gripping the back of his head. We rushed toward something big, all tongue and teeth and lips and heat.

He ripped his lips away long enough to nibble across my jaw. "I'm about to do very dirty things to you, darlin'. If you don't want it, right here, right now, say so."

"Cam." I reached for his belt, too excited to want anything but him. All of him. Right here, tucked between the buildings, only feet away from the front door to the club where people were starting to line up to enter. "I want you."

"Good." He pushed my legs off, and my boots clunked to the ground. Cam didn't wait for me, just shoved everything I wore to my ankles. There was a second for me to register being half nude in public.

Then he was on me, the sound of his belt coming loose as he jerked me up again. I kicked out of my shorts and wrapped around him.

He drove his cock inside me, once, hard, and I groaned, not caring if anyone saw me. I wanted him, all of him. I didn't even think about protection until that moment. As if he knew, he chuckled and moaned against my throat.

"I'll pull out."

And that was that. He moved, fast and hard, over and over. The rough side of the building dug into my back and the top of my ass. But I didn't care. The entire thing was so sexy, so forbidden, so hot that I came fast.

"Baby..." Cam groaned, kissing my lips and thrusting his tongue against mine.

I trembled, wracked with shocks of pleasure. But he didn't stop, pushing me past the orgasm, fucking me until I had to squeeze my eyes shut against the salacious sensation.

And then he jerked, pulling his cock all the way out of me, a sticky warmth coating the inside of my thigh.

I wrenched my lips from his, gasping, fighting to suck in the night air.

As quickly as he'd undressed me, Cam pulled a gold and black handkerchief from his pocket. I'd seen the other guys wear them so that they showed out their back pockets. The MC's colors.

He cleaned my leg, wiping himself off as well, before kneeling in front of me. He tossed the handkerchief and picked up my shorts and panties, shaking them off and holding them out so I could step into them.

From furious and rough, to aroused and undeniable, and now gentle...Cam had hit all the buttons in the last half hour. It was a whirlwind that left me dizzy but satisfied.

I zipped and buttoned my shorts while he put himself back together, still kneeling in front of me. He paused before standing, resting his face against my thighs. "I'm sorry."

"Don't be. That was fucking hot."

He shook his head, his goatee tickling the sensitive skin there. I knew what he meant, though, and stroked both sides of his head with the tips of my fingers. He was so sexy, kneeling there in front of me, everything I could ever want.

"I shouldn't have acted like that, but..." He gazed up at me, and in the shadows, I could make out the remorse on his face. "It scared me. We have to be careful. Don't say shit to anyone, don't give anyone reason to make me..."

Trailing off, he nuzzled me again then stood. "Let's go."

"Make you what, Cam?" I asked, pushing off the wall and sliding my hand into his.

He stopped at the edge of the building, long enough to light a cigarette, take a drag, and glance at me. "Hurt someone."

I would have laughed it off, but the shadows that danced in his eyes were the sort of thing nightmares were made out of. Tendrils of something unexpected skittered up my spine and I shivered despite the warmth. But not from fear, but some sort of primal excitement. Because he was speaking the truth and I wanted more of that side of him.

Almost to the bike, a woman climbed from a dark SUV and caught sight of us. She made a beeline for Cam, trailed her fingers over the patch on his chest, and winked. Cam politely shoved her hand off and kept walking.

When I glanced over my shoulder, she stood and watched us, a sad and almost wistful expression on her face. The look was a stark contrast to the rest of her. She wore a fur stole, diamond earrings winking at her ears, and a silky dress that clung to every curve in a way that was as classy as it was sexy.

She blinked once, as if really seeing me, then put on a bright smile. Then she ducked inside that club.

"Who was that?" I asked at the bike.

Cam shrugged. "One of Val's girls."

"A dancer?"

Cam chuckled. "No, darlin'. Not a dancer. She's an escort. I've seen her around before." He got really quiet, like an iron door slammed shut on his face.

"I never took you for the hooker type."

"Not me." He crushed the cigarette out under his boot. "Archer."

"Oh." That put the entire weird exchange into perspective.

At least Archer had good taste. She was beautiful.

Four

RILEY

On the way home, Cam pulled into the parking lot of a well-known chain motel. The buildings were painted bright yellow and seemed far cheerier than its run-down counterparts I'd stayed in when in California.

The rumble of another Harley grabbed my attention. Cam didn't even look up. He'd known. I should have figured when he didn't even glance, it was Merc.

He pulled up beside us, killed his engine, and they both sat in the quiet. The spectacle of the day left me sore, tired, and ready to go home. Where I'd sleep for a whole damn week.

"What's going on?"

"Three-oh-three," Cam lit a cigarette. "It's the room Archer died in. I haven't driven back this way, because I was afraid I couldn't handle seeing it alone."

"You've got us." I wrapped my arms around him and hugged him tight, laying my face against the cool leather. Merc and Cam had been friends for a long time, so it made sense that he'd roll up right then.

But I was new in Cam's life and felt honored that he would choose to have me with him at that moment. This was more of a tribute, the three of us sitting silently, than the dog and pony show the funeral had been.

We sat in silence for a long time. This reverence wasn't something I was a part of, but I was falling in love with Cam and he'd loved my father.

My heart pounded in my chest. Until then, I hadn't even thought those words. Putting a label on what I was feeling was like being pitched off a cliff into the dark unknown. I swallowed hard and looked away from the room where my father had taken his last breaths.

And I saw her again. The prostitute from the club. Her big eyes were sad as she gazed at me. She knew who we were, who I was. Then she dipped her head with respect and disappeared into a room.

I shivered.

"Let's get out of here." Cam fired the bike back up and turned us toward that dilapidated storage facility across the street, then took off toward Dry Valley and home.

Because as long as he was there, for me, it *was* home.

At home, we went to bed without talking. Nothing needed to be said. Not right now, not after the day we'd had. I couldn't profess my love for a man who lived in a world I could scarcely navigate.

But I could watch over him as he slept, fall asleep myself with the warmth of his body against mine, his arm tucked around me.

When I woke near dawn, Cam was on his back, sheets low around his middle and arm folded behind his head. But he didn't look serene and calm. His face was twisted in a grimace and his brows knitted.

When he mumbled, I rolled fully to face him and shook his shoulder.

He snatched my wrist so fast I gasped. For a moment I was back in that bathroom, him bearing down on me angrily. But before I could react, the violence evaporated as quickly as it came, and he stroked the inside of my wrist with his thumb. "Sorry. Nightmare."

"Was it bad?" Did he have them often? What were they about? It was like a chink in his armor that made him seem more human.

"It's always the same." He rolled toward me, brushed some hair from my face, and ran that same thumb over my bottom lip. "More memory than dream."

"I have those, about when my mom was sick." Since being here, they'd stopped. Now when I thought of her, it was of the good things and the parts that made me happy. "Those last few months were so hard."

"You took care of her." It was more statement than question.

"I did, I would again. I'm glad I had her while I did."

"Wish I could say the same." No humor, just a sad smile.

"Are the nightmares about her?" I could tell I'd pushed too far, watched the armor go up and his face morph into that mask he wore around Preacher and some of the others. Nothing coming in, but nothing getting out either. "I'm sorry, I shouldn't..."

"No." He pulled me to him, turning me so that my back was pressed against his chest and he spooned around me. "You deserve to know, especially if this between us is goes any further. And even if it doesn't."

He took a deep breath, his chest moving up and down against my back as he did. "There are always going to be things I can't tell you. But this...secret, is mine. This is something I can give you—for better or worse."

"Okay." This time I rubbed his arm in slow rhythmic motions meant to offer comfort. Whatever he was about to tell me was heavy. I could feel the weight of it between us.

"My mom was a junkie. Never met my dad, don't care to. She had this revolving door of assholes who would pay the bills, smack her around, and give her money for dope. She married one. He was such a douche, so I spent most of my time gone. Either at Ro's or wherever I could crash."

I saw him, a kid bouncing from place to place with nothing to call his own. I understood now why the Desert Kings and the bond they had were so important to him.

"I'm not a good man, Riley. All that shit yesterday...that's who I am. I can't promise you I'll be better, and I won't pretend that I'd change any of the shit in my past. But I was sixteen, came home and she was really high, still had the needle sticking out of her arm when I walked in. I was tired of that shit, young and mad, and couldn't deal. We had a fight, screamed at each other, and then her husband came in and said some shit. He was a cocky, skinny punk ass bitch. Mom got in between us, and they stormed out."

He trembled once, and I pulled his arms tighter around me. When he spoke, the words were threaded with tears that he wouldn't shed, with grief and shame he'd carry the rest of his life. I ached for him. "There are people who know, who knew. Archer. Preach. AP and Ro. I'm pretty sure Merc, too. But I've never said it out loud. Not to anyone."

"I'm here." Was all I could say. If he wanted to unleash his demons on me, I'd take them. Because I knew he'd slay all of mine.

"I heard something crash, her scream, and by the time I got to the back door I could hear him hitting her. There had been times when I was younger that I got knocked around trying to intervene. But I was older, stronger, meaner than I had been. We fought. I hit him and he hit me. Then I looked over and..." He sucked in a breath. "She was dying. Choking on her own blood or vomit, from the beating or the drugs, I'll never know."

My stomach lurched and my heart broke into a thousand pieces. I knew where this was going now, because I knew Cam. And I understood now why my father had taken him in, kept him safe.

"I grabbed the big ashtray from the table, this heavy one she kept change and shit in. And I beat him with it. Over and over, until he stopped moving. Then I called Ro, held mom until she got there. That's the first night I realized just how far Archer's reach was and how much I'd owe the club."

I thought back to Ro and the diner, what she'd said about mistakes she'd made. This hadn't been one. She'd protected the boy she loved the only way she knew how. "He made it go away?" Though it didn't seem possible.

Cam nodded against the back of my head. "If you want to go, Riley, I won't stop you. But I can't leave, I can never leave. The Desert Kings own me."

And that's when my heart shattered completely.

I'd always seen the world in black and white, but Cam had shown me that a gray area did exist. I'd always thought I could never be a criminal defense attorney, that representing a guilty person wasn't beyond me. But I'd defend that young man's act with every beat of my heart.

Because some people deserved it, some people didn't, and it wasn't up to me to decide.

I'm not sure when we both fell asleep. But the sun was bright and beaming through a partially opened blind when I woke. Cam snored slightly beside me and when I rolled over to look at him, he was the same beautiful boy I'd fallen asleep next to. Not the monster he believed himself to be.

He'd told me his deepest, darkest secret and I'd take it to my grave. Just like my father had done. But even that hadn't changed how I saw him, how I felt about him.

The knowledge that taking him away from here, from this life, was impossible was a different story.

When my phone sang out its cheery ringtone, I rolled over and silenced it before it could wake him. I glanced over my shoulder to see him roll onto his back and stretch. But he stayed asleep.

The number was one I'd saved, Archer's lawyer. I slid as quietly as I could from the bed and crept out onto the front porch, hoping I wouldn't wake him. I called Kimbrell back. The conversation was brief, but it sent me headfirst into a pit of anxiety.

Could I come by today? There was some stuff that needed to be handled. Of course I could. We'd read the will while I was there. No one else was necessary.

When I walked back into Cam's apartment, he was sitting on the edge of the bed, running a hand through his messy hair. I wasn't as quiet or sneaky as I'd thought.

"Hey, I'm sorry." I smiled sheepishly and walked to him.

"Good morning." He tugged me down onto his lap and kissed me. "Everything okay?"

"Yes, but no." I nuzzled my head into his neck. "Archer's lawyer wants me to come in."

"Let me take a quick shower and we can head that way." No further questioning.

When I gave him a curious glance, he lifted one shoulder lazily. "I don't like the way Preacher hounded you at the club house. Quicker I can get that shit sorted, the better I'll feel."

"I couldn't agree more."

I stood, and he grabbed my hands before I could step away from the side of the bed. "I won't let him hurt you, Riley."

The conviction in his voice made me shiver from a cold that didn't exist. I thought about what he'd told me, about his stepdad and the reason he was a Desert King. And like when he'd told me, I didn't run.

I stepped between his thighs, wrapped my arms around him, and kissed him with everything I felt. When I pulled away, breathless, I pressed my forehead to his. "I know."

Cradling my hands between his, he stroked them with his thumbs. "We got this."

I sure as hell hoped so. Because I never wanted him to let go.

Five

Riley

Cam held open the door to Kimbrell and Associates for me, our entrance heralded by the chiming of electronic bells. Though, that was the last piece of modern anything we encountered in the waiting room. Dark wood-paneled walls, surrounded by plush leather furniture, and dotted with elegant framed images of the desert and various rock formations.

Copies of Golf Digest and Good Housekeeping occupied equal amounts of space on the large, expensive looking glass topped coffee table.

The low, dulcet tones of a twenty-four-hour news channel emanated from the flat screen television mounted in the corner of the room above the tidy, inconspicuous coffee and snack cart.

When I inhaled, I was rewarded with the scent of leather, polish, books, and spiced nuts. This was the sort of place that put me right at ease. Made me think of notebooks and lectures, reminders of the world I'd had to leave behind when Mom got sick.

The life I'd imagined for myself. Until I'd met Cam, the idea of that life had been my defining characteristic. The part of me that was wholly me.

The irony of losing the loving parent, the one who'd sacrificed so much for me, was that she left me homeless. But losing the parent I'd never known, who'd never loved me enough to sacrifice his lifestyle for me, had given me the opportunity to fight for a new home. And now I wasn't so sure I wanted it.

The confusion tumbled around in my gut, making me nauseous.

I glanced at Cam as he stopped just inside the door. Without the cut covered in Desert King patches, he looked so different. No less attractive, but oddly stripped down and vulnerable. He nodded and greeted the receptionist behind the big desk in the corner opposite the television. She was discreet; I'd barely noticed her.

Without asking us to sign in, she stood and ducked through a different door before I even had time to sit on one of the couches. I perched on the edge, nervous energy making my stomach tight. Cam sat beside me, threading his long, calloused fingers through mine in my lap.

His blue eyes and soft expression said he was here for support, whatever I needed.

I'd only ever had Mom to lean on. Trusting him enough to do so was new, but warm and inviting. How could I leave that behind?

There had to be a way I could have the life I'd always imagined *and* Cam.

A friendly-looking man in his mid-forties opened the adjoining door. "Cam," he said in greeting before turning to me and extending a hand. "And you must be Riley. I'm Sam Kimbrell, I hope your day is going well. I appreciate you coming down on such short notice."

"No problem at all." I stood and shook his hand. It was warm, firm, but not rough like Cam's. Another difference in the dual lives I wanted for myself.

Cam released his grip on my other and stayed seated. "I'll be out here if you need me."

He wouldn't be like Preacher, circling like a salivating buzzard. I appreciated that as much as his stoic support.

Inside Kimbrell's office was almost the same as the waiting room. Except the walls behind his desk were floor to ceiling bookshelves filled with all sorts of law books, framed photographs of his family. But I was most surprised by the detective and cowboy novels scattered here and there.

"I think Archer read some of those. I found them in his closet." I didn't know what else to say. I was nervous, and the connection seemed a way to ease into the conversation.

He smiled warmly. "Yeah, he bought me one of those after we talked about books one day." He reached behind himself and pulled a hardback copy from a shelf.

I read the spine. "*The Walking Drum*, by *Louis L'Amour*."

"Means a lot more now." He slid it back into place. "I'm sorry that we're meeting under these circumstances. He told me you were looking into going to law school. Seems we have some things in common."

Shock left me cold. Archer had known I was aiming for law school? *But how...*

And if he knew that, why hadn't he helped when Mom got sick, when they were both still alive?

I'm not sure what Kimbrell said next, but I tilted my head as if I listened intently. When I finally tuned in through my astonishment, he was reading through a list of Archer's assets.

"The short of it, everything is yours except the land and the buildings the Desert Kings use—he left that to the club, both his Harleys to Cameron Savage, and the house—to you *and* Cam."

"Us both?" That was weird, playing match maker from the grave.

"He expressed interest that Cam not be kicked out as soon as your mother decided to sell. He wrote this before her passing." He added the last part when I made a face.

Then he rattled off the liquid assets and cash on hand, the whole of it more than enough to give me a good start if I liquidated everything. But by no means enough to send Preacher buzzing around like the vulturous creep he was.

"There's a list of his bills. As Executor of the estate, I'll handle most of it as it goes through the probate process, but everything will be documented. I needed you to sign a few things, since you're his heir." He slid papers to me.

I listened as he explained what each was. I liked the way he spoke, making things simple without watering them down and making me feel stupid.

The signing was the easy part.

"In this"—he waved a fat, manilla envelope in front of him—"I've put a list of the bills and assets, so you have everything in writing. Deeds, titles, and the like will come later. He also wrote some letters, personal documents, things like that. They are in here and it's your discretion to distribute them all."

"Oh." That was heavy. I took the envelope.

As he walked me to the door, he gave me a sad smile. "Working for your dad gave me a new outlook on a certain type of people. He shook up my world view. I'll never forget him for that, and his loss is felt deeply."

Boy, did I know that feeling. I smiled back. "Thank you."

"What type of law are you considering?"

And for the first time, I said what I'd been thinking out loud. "Criminal. I'd like to be a defense attorney."

"You're in the right place for that." He chuckled as he led me back out to Cam.

Archer had shaken up my world view. Maybe for the better.

***

We'd driven the blacked-out pickup I'd barely seen leave the garage behind Archer's place. I studied him again, as all the questions about my dad tumbled around in my brain, all the things Cam couldn't answer.

This was the first time I'd seen him drive something other than the bike. He was comfortable, one arm draped over the wheel, his face relaxed. Yet, he looked different in the black t-shirt with a faded Desert King's logo on the front right chest.

"Where's the cut?" That was a question he could answer and one that broke the silence.

There was a slight hesitation, like he had to shake himself out of his thoughts, before he glanced at me. "Don't wear them in cars, that sort of shit. Nothing can touch the patch." Then he gave me a flirty grin and wink. "Except you, maybe. If you're lucky."

"That all you want me to touch?" I stretched across the console and kissed the warm skin on the side of his neck.

"Keep that up, and I'll definitely have something you can touch."

I ran my hand across his groin and found proof that he wasn't lying stretching against his jeans.

He swatted my hand away with a chuckle as we pulled into the diner where I'd first met Ro. "If we weren't in public, darlin', I'd have you naked with your legs over my shoulders. Not just touching you, all the way inside you."

He was kissing me as he put the truck in park. His tongue was rough against mine, claiming me, reminding me that if we weren't in a public parking lot he'd have me on the ground exactly like he'd threatened.

Damn. It wasn't Cam battling back the desire when we sat down in a familiar booth.

Before the other waitress could offer us menus, Ro rushed over. This time, she pulled me out of the booth for a tight hug, too. Cam greeted her as if he was happy to see her, as if he didn't know all the things he knew. His poker face was strong.

Not strong enough, though, because Ro noticed too. Rubbing her lips together, she worried her apron with both hands as she left us to get drinks.

I sat across from him, my stomach rumbling. "He left you his bikes," I said as I skimmed the menu Ro had left behind.

He didn't say anything at first, just leaned back and stretched an arm over the back of the booth and gazed out the window. I'm sure he was curious about what the lawyer said, but all of this had a larger effect on him than me.

Plus, he was still grieving. I second guessed even saying anything to him.

"I thought you might like that. I didn't mean to say something to hurt you." I worried I had by the darkness in his eyes.

"You didn't." He leaned forward and wrapped a hand around my wrist, massaging my pulse with his thumb. "I'll sign everything back over to you."

"What the hell am I going to do with a motorcycle, Cam?" I widened my eyes and made a face. "Much less two. That's ridiculous. You were a big part of his life. You deserve that."

"Sell them," he offered. He relaxed, and the creases at the corner of his eyes evaporated.

"There's some money and property, but nothing to make Preacher so sketchy." That bothered me. The way the other man hovered was as if I'd get some huge windfall. "And it would take time to sell off any of that."

He didn't immediately reply, like he was tossing around the idea of what to tell me and what not—more secrets piling up between us. Just when I thought I knew him, there was another brick in his wall.

"Some of that is Ro's place, the house, the clubhouse, and some rentals." He interjected, well acquainted with Archer's life. Living in the now, it was easy to forget he'd been here long before I was. That's why he didn't ask about what the lawyer had to say—he already knew what Archer's plans had been.

"The Kings get the clubhouse and the land. You and I split the house."

He barked a short laugh as Ro came back to take our order but said nothing else about it. As we ate lunch, Cam changed the subject, talked about mundane things. I was thankful for that. The past few days had been a lot to process. Hell, the past few weeks had been a whirlwind of chaos.

We ate, chatted with Ro, and by the time we were done, he was my Cam again. I liked it better when he was easy, sexy. Made it easier to forget all the bullshit.

He lit a cigarette as we stepped out into the afternoon sun.

"Cam," Ro followed. "We should talk soon."

"Nothing to talk about." He took a drag and put his back to her as he strolled toward the truck. "You're old enough to know what you're playing at."

The lines on her face pulled tight, distraught. Cam's opinion mattered a great deal to her. I wanted to smack him in the back, tell him to turn around and talk to her. She shook her head slowly, warning me not to get involved.

I gave her a quick, tight hug and jogged after him.

"What was that all about?" I asked as I climbed in the truck and he drove from the parking lot.

"She's screwing around with Preacher." Just like that, the easiness was gone, and he'd retreated into the darkness that always seemed to shadow his eyes.

That dollop of information was enough of a shock to make the ride home silent.

The thing with Cam was if we were alone for longer than five minutes, we couldn't keep our hands off each other. I could be angry, scared, mad, and if left to our own devices, we'd be all over each other, regardless.

No conversation in the truck, but with one quick grin in the kitchen, he had me up on the counter, himself firmly between my thighs...inside me. My leggings and panties on the floor near Cam's shirt. He kissed me after, long and slow and full of all the confusing emotions that passed between us.

I was breathless, my body all tingly, when he finally broke away to catch his breath. Each time we kissed, I expected something to change, but it didn't. Each one was as hot, as tempting, as the first. My knees went a little weak and my stomach flipped.

The quiet knock on the back door was startling, breaking through the haze of lust and sex. We weren't expecting anyone.

Cam released me and glanced out the window over the sink. He fastened his pants and tugged on his shirt as he walked to the door. He was all business now, back straight and jaw tight. "It's Kenna."

Panic laced through me and pushed all the other feelings away. Kenna had grown on me. Her boyfriend had not. I worried about her, was protective of her. I hurriedly yanked on my clothes, brushed my hair from my face, and pushed past Cam as he opened the door.

"You okay?" My voice was strained, but I tried not to squeak. I was always ready for the next shoe to drop and hoped she hadn't got caught in our crossfire.

She blinked, smiled, then glanced over her shoulder, nervously shifting around like a tiny, scared kitten, as if someone might be watching her. The only thing behind her was her sporty little black pickup parked beside Cam's bike. No monsters lurking...that I could see.

"Oh yeah, I'm good ..." She worried her lip like she should say more but didn't know if she could.

Cam took a step back, pulled me with him, and tucked me to his side, making room for her to come in and gesturing for her to do so. "Need something from me?"

Relief loosened the tension in her expression. "Yeah, I guess... maybe... I sort of need to..." She took a deep breath. "No, there's for sure something I need to tell you."

It was obvious my presence was causing her an issue. Which meant whatever she had to say was about the Kings. Her divided loyalty—between me and the club—was distressing. There was no reason for that.

"I'm going to hop in the shower." I kissed Cam's cheek and sent her what I hoped was a soothing look.

Kenna smiled gratefully and walked a small circle around the kitchen table. Curious or not, I left them to it. My loyalties weren't divided. I loved them both.

I hadn't told him yet, but there was no denying what my feelings were.

Something else to leave my knees weak.

Six

CAM

She didn't sit; she paced the kitchen like a tiny ball of energy. If she could bounce against the walls, she might have.

"Rip the bandage off; it's easier that way," I said, breaking up weed into a blunt shell as the water kicked on in the shower on the other side of the wall. "Say what's on your mind. It's just you and me."

Kenna stopped, blinked, and wrapped her arms around herself.

"You don't need to be afraid of me; I'm not going to hurt you." And I meant it. There were clear lines in my mind. Things I didn't do, refused to cross.

Archer had taught me to take care of my own.

"I was going to talk to David first, run it by him, but..."

Her stepdad had sat at the table before and been a patched member of the Desert Kings for years. Archer had trusted him.

"But he's never liked Ghost and after what happened to you and Riley with the peckerwoods"—she chewed her bottom lip and refused to look up at me—"I'm not trying to get anyone in trouble. But the other day... that scared me. Riley, you, somebody could have been hurt."

"It's just me and you. What you say here, I'll never say who told me."

Kenna's loyalty had been to the Kings since she was a kid. Same as mine. I'd honor that and protect her. Even if he had no part in Archer's death, Preacher had forgotten that part of being a Desert King.

I leaned against the counter and lit the blunt. I'd never light a cigarette in Archer's house, but it wasn't past me to smoke some weed in the kitchen. And from what I saw, Kenna needed it.

"Yesterday, I thought I recognized one of the trucks that was following you. Puck mentioned finding out exactly who was driving, and I made it a point to keep my eyes open." She took a long inhale of the blunt I handed her, held it, then blew it out before continuing. "Anyway, Ghost and I kind of got into it last night, and I went to bed before him. But I was too mad to sleep, so when I heard a woman laugh I thought maybe Ghost was trying to pull something and I went to the window."

We passed the blunt back and forth again. My nerves were getting more and more amped by the minute. I had a feeling where this was going. I'd been putting stuff together on my own. Kenna loosened a little and sat at the kitchen table closest to me.

"I looked outside and there was that same damn truck. I could see straight through the windshield. It was Jessica—you know, Puck's ex?" When I nodded, she continued. "She was with Kyle Haynes, Wanda's youngest son. I know because sometimes Ghost sells weed and shit to them. I thought that's what he might be doing, but then he handed Kyle a fat roll of cash."

She swallowed hard, took another hit, handed it back to me, and closed her eyes against the emotion I could plainly hear in her voice. Bringing this to me cost her a great deal. I wouldn't forget that.

"Ghost know you saw them?" Proof the guy was an idiot, having them come to his damn house... with her there. Or maybe he hadn't had a choice—Preach was his sponsor.

I rubbed at the prickling itch on the back of my neck.

She shook her head. "I pretended to be asleep when he came back in. I was on my way to work when I stopped here. He's still in bed. I didn't go to Preacher because..." She let it trail off.

Smart girl. If Ghost was paying off the Hayneses, then Preacher knew all about it.

Mother fucker.

"Keep this on the down low, don't even say anything to David, and I'll keep the blow back off you as much as I can."

She nodded. "Thanks."

"Don't even tell Puck."

She babysat his kid a lot. But had been running around behind him like a lost puppy for years.

"And remember, you don't have to be Ghost's ole lady." She had better options. "You're a friend, regardless."

She smiled a sad little smile as Riley walked back in, and I stubbed out the roach in the sink. Riley's hair was damp, and she smelled fucking delicious. I wanted her now, even this pissed off, when I'd just had her, still smelled of her.

"Thanks. You did the right thing."

"You're welcome." She turned to Riley, her usual bubbly self, having handed her burden to me. "You coming to Desert Lights?"

Shit. I'd forgotten. Despite everything that had happened, life continued to roll on.

Riley's brow lifted. "I don't know what that even is."

"Seriously, Cam?" Kenna rolled her big eyes. "Stop sucking her face and start telling her about the cool stuff."

Riley laughed.

"It's a big rave in the desert, a joint thing by a bunch of DJs and fraternities and shit. Lasts for two days. The Desert Kings run security on it since it's in Dry Valley. Also means we get in free." She rushed on. "I can do your hair. We can match. Dylan won't ever go with me and my friend that usually goes is going to be out of town."

Riley seemed genuinely interested. The way her face lit up and she leaned in told me I'd be taking her with me. "I wouldn't turn down a chance to see you in something slutty, partying in the desert."

She grinned, swatted at me with the back of her hand, as they launched into a conversation of glitter and outfits and a good time. Riley deserved that. She hadn't had many lately. This was something I could give her, happily.

Leaving them to it, I stepped outside and called the only man I trusted with the information Kenna had just given me to have him meet me at the clubhouse later.

***

The clubhouse was mostly empty, a fact I was thankful for. It was too early in the day for even Dylan to be there working the bar. Only a few old timers who didn't have day jobs hung around, playing cards at a corner table. I tossed a two fingered wave and made for the stairs.

Merc was already on the roof when I opened the top door.

"Archer's office." He half smiled, kind of sad. "Didn't know being up here would hit me so hard."

"Every time." I agreed.

I went to the ledge he peered over. The desert stretched out before us all the way to the mountains in the distance. This was where I'd been the first time I'd realized how much I wanted to kiss Riley Bowman.

It was also where I stood the night Archer offered me an out, a life not spent behind bars. Even signing a deal with the devil it was one hell of a view.

Full circle.

"Someone saw one of the peckerwood's trucks at Ghost's place after we ran them out of here." I didn't say who. I'd keep that secret for Kenna.

"Sure it was theirs?"

"Yeah. Recognized one of Wanda's boys driving."

Merc didn't say much at first. "Did you see any of the main crew after the chase?"

"Nah, not Dustin or Kyle. I wouldn't know any of the others. Those fuckers breed like white trash rabbits." Wanda had at least three sons and a slew of cousins. Inbred fuckers.

He snorted. "No shit. Have you told anyone else?"

What he didn't say, was that this could shake out two ways—Preacher didn't know and Ghost is done.

Or Preacher knew.

"All hell would break loose," Merc said, correctly reading my silence in a way only he could.

"Even worse if I prove he killed Archer." If it took everything in me, I'd damn sure do that—to protect Riley. And my club.

Merc sucked in a breath between his teeth.

It was the first time I'd said it out loud. *No going back now.*

"We have to move carefully." His voice was low. I didn't have to look at him to know he was running all the scenarios through his head.

His brain wasn't wired like everyone else's. That wasn't the army's doing—that's what made him so good at what he did for them. "Find out how many we've got at the table."

I laughed without humor. "Never thought I'd see the Desert Kings dividing loyalties like this."

"Bound to happen one day." Matter of fact, much like his dad.

Might not surprise Merc, but it turned me inside out. The Desert Kings were the only security I'd ever known; the only real family I'd ever had. I could lose that forever. There was a time where this very thing had been my biggest fear. Then I'd met Riley...

"You can't let him get to you. No mouthing off to him when he baits you." Merc spit into the pebbled rocks on the roof, then raked his boot across to cover them. "Don't let anyone see him rile you."

"I can't make any promises when it comes to her." I didn't have to say who, didn't have to hide the emotion in my voice.

"He knows she's your trigger. He'll keep going for it."

Merc wasn't wrong. We both turned back to the door emblazoned with the MC logo.

"We don't make any moves until after the fight." I told him. That put two events between us and the peckerwood incident. "Maybe give Ghost a shake and see what he drops."

Merc grunted in agreement. "I'll scope out the rest of the table."

We needed to find out who was in Preacher's back pocket and who would rock with us.

"I don't think he'll do anything until we ratify the table, vote on the probies. But..." He slapped a hand on my shoulder. "Watch your back, brother."

I'd be watching all of our backs. The Kings still meant something to me. And I had a target, something to shoot for. And for the first time since Archer died, I had the beginnings of a plan.

"The big vote is months out. I don't have that sort of time, brother." I caught his gaze and held it, letting him read how heavily I carried this shit.

"Ride or die." Merc held out a fist.

I rapped my knuckles against his.

My phone dinged before he'd made it across the roof. I checked the message since it was from Riley. The anger I'd quieted came charging in, hot, violent, and ready to rip a grown man to shreds with my bare hands. Everything inside me flashed white hot.

"That fucker is at my house." Not Archer's, not Riley's. I had no right, except I did. She was *mine*.

I glanced up from the phone and all around me everything was red. From the sunset or the rage, I couldn't tell. Maybe both.

"Easy," Merc warned, stopping in the doorway and blocking my exit. "Watch that trigger. Jester is there. He won't let anything happen to her."

I wasn't so convinced and shoved him out of the way. He followed me down the stairs.

"Stay out of it." I jabbed a finger at him when he tried to duck in front of me again. The old timers looked up, grew bored quickly, and looked away.

Merc held up both hands in surrender and stopped at the bottom of the steps, knowing how far to push. I didn't doubt he fired off a text to Jester as soon as I was out the front door.

I didn't care. All that mattered was getting to Riley.

Seven

Riley

Kenna only stayed long enough to fuss through what clothes I had, deem none of them Desert Lights appropriate, and hug me tight before leaving. Whatever she'd had to talk to Cam about had been a big deal. He'd left right after, his expression so serious I was concerned.

But I didn't ask her. Not because I wasn't curious, I was. I respected her too much. I had to trust that if I needed to know, Cam would tell me.

I was more concerned with the shadows that haunted his features when he'd left for the clubhouse. Not that he'd left me here alone. Jester and his adorable younger brother were playing cards on the carport.

They looked up when I walked out, the younger laying his cards face down on the table and standing to shake my hand. "Bennett Vaughn, nice to meet you."

The facial structure was strikingly similar to Jester's. High, sharp cheekbones, and a wide, sculpted mouth. The eyes were different. A smoky blue, almost gray, and his hair a darker brown than his older brother's dirty blond. A shock of it kept falling in his eyes.

He was pretty, but on further inspection, his bottom lip was swollen and the knuckles on the hand I shook were covered in scabs.

"Jester, it's not polite to smack your little brother around," I commented as I sat at the table with them. It seemed rude to just hide in the house, especially now that I'd spent time with Jester. But I'd heard at The Black Cat that his brother also fought. I hadn't expected him to be this young. He couldn't even be old enough to drink alcohol.

He snorted, kicked back in his chair. "I've never hit the little bastard outside of sparring. He had a fight up in Reno last weekend. Dude was twice his size, but he still put him on his ass."

With a sheepish grin, Bennett added, "Big doesn't do much good when you can't grapple and don't put weight behind your punches. It wasn't a fair fight, but I let him get a few knocks in, so he didn't feel too bad about getting his ass kicked."

"Have you both always fought?"

"Our Dad was a boxer back in the day. Kind of a family tradition. We grew up in a ring," Bennett told me easily, happy to talk about something he loved.

I was happy to oblige him with more questions, but shook my head no when Jester offered to deal me in. "Is it the violence that is so enticing, or is it just another adrenaline rush like riding the bike?"

They exchanged one of those glances that said they'd both had the exact same thought at the same time, and the only person in the world to find it as funny as they did was each other. Then they both laughed.

Bennett answered. "The fighting is technical. Lots of training. Mixed Martial Arts requires a foundation in several fighting styles.

Riding a bike is going as fast as you can, with no training, and hoping you don't die."

Jester's eye roll was massive. "Or it is when you ride." He leaned into me, talking in a fake conspiratorial whisper. "There's a reason we call him Crash. As in Crash Test Dummy."

"I'm buying a Suzuki GSXR one thousand."

Jester snorted, then smacked his brother's hand with the cards he held. "Stick to the ring, kid."

"Watch me. You used to love a sport bike."

"That was then," Jester plucked a card from the deck on the table, then fanned out the cards in his hand and stuck it between two.

"Why not anymore?" Genuine curiosity perked me up. I hadn't seen any of the guys ride anything other than a Harley.

"Desert Kings ride Harleys. That's it." He shrugged.

"It's patch in, but I'm not swearing off *fast* bikes."

"You're going to get your damn self killed." The older Vaughn turned to me, sunlight playing off the tattoos that ran all the way up his throat. "He rode motocross for years, tries to treat a Harley like that. Had my old crotch rocket for a while, drove it off a bridge—and it was just a pissy five hundred. Amazing the little fucker's still alive," he said with a mix of repressed fear and brotherly appreciation.

Bennett smiled proudly. "I'm still here."

Jester shook his head and laid out his cards. "Gin, bitch."

They were like that, back and forth with the ease of brothers—of two young men that had spent their lives taking care of each other. I'd been right, Bennett wasn't even old enough to buy alcohol. Nineteen, five years younger than his brother.

Neither seemed like outlaws. They weren't the scary men lurking in the shadows that Mom had warned me about. They were just brothers, playing cards one evening. Their presence made me feel secure, safe, as much from the normalcy in their interactions as anything else.

***

In my room—I thought of it less and less as Archer's guestroom—I sat on the bed and opened the envelope the lawyer had given me. I'd left Jester and Bennett out back, cutting up and giving each other shit. I didn't feel so alone whenever their chatter flitted in through the partially opened window.

But I was alone enough to go over the things Archer had left to me. For the first time in months, I didn't feel like the rug was about to be jerked from beneath me. The stories Mom had told me about my father and the men around him no longer jived with what I knew the Desert Kings to be.

It was a family, one that might blur the lines between legal and illegal from time to time, but they took care of their own—took care of an entire town.

Archer hadn't been the boogeyman. He'd saved Cam and he'd saved me.

I didn't open the letter for Cam, but set it aside and dug for another, looking for one for me.

A folded piece of paper with the name Preacher scrawled across the front fell into my lap. Since it wasn't in an envelope like Cam's, I unfolded it. Two words written in that same writing took up most of the space.

You lose.

A knot lodged in my throat, expanded and constricted, forcing my breaths to come in broken bursts. A thrumming, static throb grew in my ears, consuming all other sound. Whatever Preacher was playing at—Archer had been too.

When I heard Preacher's voice, I blinked to make sure I wasn't stuck in some weird, waking nightmare. I hadn't heard his bike pull up. Why was he here?

Still clutching Archer's letter to him, I tiptoed into the kitchen and peeked out the window over the sink. He was there, chatting up Jester and Bennett. The creepy, ick inducing feel crept up my spine and left me cold and a little nauseous.

I texted Cam that Preacher was at the house. His response was immediate.

Stay inside or with Jester. I'm on my way.

Still hidden in the shadows of the kitchen, I eavesdropped. It wasn't until I heard him tell Jester he could cut out that I stepped out the back door.

"Hey Jester, can I talk to you?" Keeping the panic from my voice had taken all I had.

"He's just leaving, hon. They need to be training for the big fight. Not babysitting Cam's ole lady."

Jester ignored him, his face no longer affable and charming, but quiet and eerily calm as he watched me. "Nah, it's cool." He stood, walked to the steps, and tossed his arm over my shoulder. With an ease of a man comfortable around women, he led me inside.

Then, as if he realized he was acting out of character, he cut a wide, toothy smile. "What Cam don't know won't hurt him."

Then he winked over his shoulder at Preacher.

"Jesus." His brother tossed his cards down and rubbed a hand over his half-disgusted expression.

Preacher faltered long enough for us to take advantage and duck back into the kitchen, Jester shutting the door. We left him outside with Bennett.

Having dealt with his real flirtations, I hadn't bought the act and wasn't surprised when he dropped his arm and sobered as soon as we were out of earshot.

"What's up?"

I glanced out at Preacher, he was glaring at the door. I scooted farther across the kitchen, ensuring he couldn't see me. "I don't want to be alone with him."

If I'd expected him to scoff or laugh that off, I'd have been disappointed.

"I'm not going to pretend I know what's going on. But I'm not leaving any woman alone if she's uncomfortable. Especially not a friend or a friend's ole lady."

No laughing, no joking, just matter of fact.

"Thanks." I smiled at him as he leaned against the living room doorframe. "Is your brother okay?"

Outside, Preacher grumpily bitched at Bennett, though this time I couldn't make out what he was saying.

"He's fine. He's a tough son of a bitch." Then he nodded toward them. "What's the old fuck want, anyway?"

"I don't know." I glanced down at the letter in my hand, folded it neatly and held it close. "Maybe he found out I saw Archer's lawyer today."

"He's probably panicked about the clubhouse. It's a concern some of the guys have brought up."

I thought about Archer's letter. There had to be something else.

"It belongs to the Club. Archer had a bunch of business documents lined up. He left the land and the building to the Desert Kings." It shouldn't be a secret; it wasn't something any of them needed to worry about.

Jester whistled. "You okay with that?"

"What would I do with it?" I snorted. "This is more than fair."

He didn't have a chance to respond before Preacher stepped through the back door without invitation. "You good in here?"

Until you showed up. "Sure."

"How'd it go today?" He shuffled the bulk of himself into the kitchen between Jester and me.

Over his shoulder, Jester gave an almost imperceptible shake of his head. I didn't ask how he'd known. "Fine."

You lose. I clutched the letter to my chest. What game had Archer been playing at?

"What's that?" He eyed it. "Just something I was working on." I lied.

"Get everything settled?" He loomed over me.

"There are some bills to pay." The rest wasn't any of his business. "Kimbrell is the executor and handling most everything."

"Nothing interesting, then? No more surprise children popping up?" He chuckled like his joke was funny.

"I wasn't a surprise to those of you who knew," I said, flat and without emotion.

Jester watched intently, face intense and jaw tight. Such a different look for him that I got chills. A reminder that Cam wasn't the only dangerous one.

I moved around Preacher, closer to Jester's side of the kitchen, almost gagging on the spicy cologne he wore far too much of. I had to bump into him to force him to step back so that I could open the fridge. I was petty enough that I pulled out a single beer and passed it to Jester.

And I adored him, because he popped the top and took a long swallow.

In the distance the roar of an angry Harley approached—fast. The closer the sound got, the antsier Preacher became.

"I was just making sure you didn't need anything and everything was being taken care of."

"Kimbrell is a pretty competent guy. I don't foresee any issues."

Obvious annoyance flashed in his eyes beneath bushy eyebrows.

"Is there anything else you need?" I kept my voice cool, calm. Inside, I was anything but. Even my trust in Jester was fragile.

I needed Cam.

I positioned myself near the kitchen drawer that housed the loaded pistol. The roar of the Harley engine was almost on top of us now. He'd be thundering up the driveway any minute. Because it wasn't just any bike, I knew that sound as well as the beat of my heart. I could pick it out any of them.

Cam.

The older man switched tactics once he realized he would get nowhere before Cam got here, and I wasn't so easily intimidated.

"You really want that alone time with Corey here, huh?" He insinuated with a perverse waggle of those caterpillar eyebrows. "Jumping to a new bike already."

Out of the corner of my eye, I watched Cam hop off his in one smooth motion as he shut it off.

"What the fuck, Preacher?" Jester spat. This time he didn't bother hiding his disgust with the older man.

I sneered. "If you are implying I would ever have sex with anyone other than Cam—"

"You'd be out of fucking line." Cam's voice, sharp as a razor, cut me off.

Preacher made a show or rolling his eyes and shaking his head, like we'd overreacted. "I was teasing." He didn't turn to Cam, instead stared me down. As if he telling me I'd pay for this.

Cam went through him with a hard shoulder. He knocked the older man off balance. When he did, Preacher stumbled, red faced and angry. Then lifted his arm like he would punch Cam. Jester jumped in between.

Cam didn't even flinch.

"Lets go have a beer and talk to the kid about the fight." He grabbed a second one from the fridge. Friendly arm around Preacher this time.

The older man was tall, but it wasn't until then I realize Jester was about the same height. The younger man didn't use his stature to intimidate. Didn't need to.

Cam turned to Preacher with a hard, blue-eyed glare.

There was a moment of hesitation in the older man. With a sneer, Cam turned his back on him to kiss me. Preacher turned and stomped out with Jester.

"I'm going to fuck him up if he comes near you again," he growled, pulling me against his chest and holding me.

I hugged him tight, letting all the bravado I'd built up leak out. I didn't have to hold it all together when Cam was here.

"He knew I went to the lawyer. Did you tell anyone?"

Cam stiffened. "No. Maybe Ro overheard something."

If she told, it would break his heart.

Eight

CAM

The desire to smash my fist into Preacher's smug face was almost as strong as the drive to protect Riley. From him, from everyone. Whatever it took, even if that meant reining in the violence that came with my temper.

That savagery raged, clawing at the inside of my chest. Just touching her didn't quiet it. But that beast inside craved two things: violence and Riley Bowman.

Taking her when I felt like this, when I couldn't control myself... would it be too much? Scare her away? Hurt her? I couldn't be sure. So I focused on the other side, the gnawing, growling part that craved blood.

How many times had I been in handcuffs because of this? But then I'd never had something worth fighting for.

She had me so flipped around I couldn't tell which end was up.

"I didn't tell anyone, Cam. The only people who knew Kimbrell called me were you and him, maybe the receptionist. No one else."

"I believe you." I rubbed the back of my neck to keep from jerking her pants off and bending her over the nearest surface. "We need to get you a burner phone. I'll switch mine again, make sure he's not tracking them."

"Were we followed?" Her hazel eyes were big.

"Nah, I'd have noticed. Especially since the shit with the pecker-woods." But someone had noticed we were there. Or had overheard us talking about it. The pitch in my stomach brought bile up the back of my throat.

I trusted very few people. One of those would have been the only person to overhear. *Ro.*

"Think it had anything to do with this?" She sat on the bed, her legs tucked under her, and pulled a piece of paper out of a large manila envelope. "The lawyer said it came from Archer."

She busied herself dumping out the rest of the contents. I focused on the note she'd handed me. The handwriting was so familiar it was like being smacked in the face by a ghost. The heat of anger leveled off to a simmer, chilled by the cold rush of grief.

On the outside of paper Preacher's name was scrawled. I unfolded the crumpled piece of paper, the one Riley had held in the kitchen.

"He wrote it," I confirmed for her, before unfolding it.

You lose.

But what had Preacher lost? So far, he had the table and the power. Sounded like what the bastard would count as a win.

He'd never have Riley. I'd die first.

"Things were tense for a while before Archer died." Between the two of them. Preacher pushing and Archer throwing up a damn cement wall.

"As openly hostile as you and Preacher are now?" She had a way of asking questions that made people want to answer them. And left little room to squirrel your way around the answer. She was already a damn good lawyer.

I snorted. "I haven't smashed his face in yet."

"That would be all out war, not hostility."

I didn't disagree. "Which is why I haven't done it...*yet.*"

Club business wasn't something I should be talking about, not to her or anyone outside of the table. But with this, Riley was the only person I trusted outside of Merc. Hell, maybe even more.

She was quiet for a while. I laid across the foot of the bed, staring at the grooves in the paper left behind by Archer's pen. The gentle sound of Riley riffling through the paperwork Kimbrell had given her the only sound aside from my breathing.

When I couldn't stand the stillness. I stood and prowled the bedroom that used to be mine. She'd slowly expanded in that space, and it was now filled with things that would forever remind me of her. Sexy little boots in the corner, a pink hairbrush on the nightstand. Her perfumes and lotions on the dresser, her jacket hanging on the back of the chair.

And the one that made me sick if I thought about it too long—her suitcases in the corner near the closet.

"Do you really think Preacher killed him?" Her voice broke through my thoughts.

"Before? I wouldn't have thought he had the balls. But now, yeah." I stopped at the foot of the bed.

"Are you sure, or is that just easier to believe than the alternative?" The concern in her eyes made my heart stutter.

"Archer damn sure didn't kill himself." It was important to me that she knew that. That Riley understood he had too much to live for, even her. Would he have reached out now that her mom was gone? Definitely. I knew it in my soul. Just like I knew he was betting on my protecting her until this was over.

"Who'd have the most to gain?"

"On paper," I swore as soon as I thought about it. "Me."

I couldn't even look at her then. She'd come to that conclusion herself, eventually. And this was the real reason I didn't go after Preacher without all the facts. Because he was going to come for me first.

Riley scoffed. "And you think I'd believe that?"

"I get the house, I get the bikes, I get you, I get a bigger position in the MC. That's more than anyone else." Turning to face her, I leaned down on the bed, arms out, resting all my weight on the hands I'd balled into fists. "Darlin', if I go for Preach, he's going to make that sound real convincing."

"And it kills you, every day." She crawled to me, on her hands and knees, nose to nose. "I can see it, feel it. Because I know what that loneliness feels like. Looking at your life and seeing the future empty is scary as fuck. No, you had nothing to do with his death. You loved him too much." There was a conviction in her voice that only Archer could have held for me.

But there was something else too, a pain. The understanding we had for each other was because we both knew what it was like to face that dark, lonely road.

God, I was in love with her.

She'd glanced down to where my fists pitted the comforter. "Look at me, darlin'." I cradled her cheek and brought her gaze to. "You're not alone anymore."

I laid my forehead against hers and closed my eyes, willing her to understand, to feel what I was feeling. Because I couldn't say it, not yet. Not when she was leaving me soon.

I'd never given anyone that much power to hurt me, to control me.

"Neither are you." She whispered.

And I was giving it to her, all wrapped up in barbed wire and razor blades.

"Fuck." I stood back from her, needing to breathe on my own for a minute before telling her.

"Here, this one is for you." She rocked back on her haunches and handed me an envelope. My full first name was written across the stark white paper in Archer's printed scrawl. The envelope was thick, as if he'd stuffed multiple pages into it.

Emotion choked me so hard, I had to force a swallow and step back. I shoved the letter in my back pocket. I'd read it later. Or not, I wasn't sure.

***

Most of my adult life I'd spent every night at the clubhouse until late, often sleeping in the room upstairs that I'd fucked Riley in. A lot of times I didn't stay up there alone. Home had been a depressing place, cold and lonely. I hadn't even called Archer's place or my apartment home, hadn't ever called anywhere home.

Then there was Riley.

I didn't want to share her, didn't want to keep her all night at the club house and party. I didn't want to drink and smoke weed until the darkness didn't matter.

I wanted to come home to her, lose myself inside her, and sleep with her pressed against me. Then wake up and do it all again.

Because I'd always done what the fuck I wanted, I'd done just that every goddamned day. I didn't stroll into the clubhouse until almost noon the day of the Dry Valley Desert Lights. Security was mine and Puck's gig had been before Archer and still was.

Preacher wasn't there. My job or not, he should have been. AP was there and marked that absence.

"You piss El Presidente off, son?"

"Man..." Jester trailed off with a half laugh, hitting a blunt and passing it to me. "Fucking Preach's got a hard-on for Cam's ole lady. All up her ass at Archer's last night, Cam smacked him down a few pegs."

AP frowned, his dark eyebrows coming together, drawing more attention to the silver threading his hair. "What did you say?"

"Not shit." I took a long hit and passed it to Merc, who was sitting by his dad.

"Watch yourself." But that was the only warning I got. Archer would have pulled me to the side, laid it all out. AP wasn't that way; he expected me to know.

I did. We all did.

Drop Top waddled in not long after, looking like either his hemorrhoids or his ole lady's bitching had kept him up all night. He smacked a roll of paper onto the large table in Chapel, unrolling it and stretching it out. "Here's your map, brother. I marked off all the stages and entrances. Where they want our main station set up." He pointed to each place.

"Show me where you want me putting people."

I did so, working it to keep the guys that could best handle themselves with those who couldn't, and dispersing the other men from the other charters in with our guys. Desert Lights was too big just for us, I had Kings coming in from several states. All shit I'd set up with Archer before he died.

I made one change. I stuck Preacher and his cronies as far away from me as I could. My adrenaline would already be high, didn't need to be worried about him all night.

"Here we go boys." Jester dropped a black backpack on the free end of the table, unzipped it, and tossed out bags of blue and purple pills. Then a few bags of white powder. "Preacher's boy, Ghost, has the weed." Then he grinned. "Wouldn't fit in my backpack, made the little fucker drive Preacher's old beater car."

It wasn't just the fee we charged to run security. This would be the only club sanctioned event where we openly provided the party favors. We knew where it came from and could control how much came in and to who it went to. Plus, the Kings made a killing. Might have been one of Preacher's only good ideas in the past few decades.

, Ghost was sitting at the bar, likely waiting on Preacher. His sponsor hadn't managed to make any of the meeting—leaving texted excuses. The other guys wondered why—I didn't.

He was avoiding me.

The information Kenna gave me burned in my chest. Ghost was no criminal mastermind. Kid could barely shake out a quarter pound of weed. Nah, Preacher had been the one to do that. But had he done it to prove a point to me about Riley? Or was it something else?

My anger over the danger he'd put her in boiled over into irritation for the little bitch's hand in it. Preacher might have put him up to hiring the peckerwoods to come for me—but he'd still done it.

Ghost could have made the same move Kenna did. He didn't.

I'd never been a bully, but I was a cocky son of a bitch. I lit a cigarette and let my attitude roll free as I approached the bar. The clubhouse was filling up, guys rolling in from other charters for the weekend.

With this many eyes on us, I couldn't strike at Preacher. Ghost's bitch ass was fair game. Chin up, ready for a fight, I forced a grin with as much arrogance as I could muster.

Nothing about Ghost was intimidating. The scrawny bastard had gone for it with the short mohawk and ghost flame tattoos on each side of his head. He'd missed.

He was a skinny prick in oversized clothes that hadn't ever done shit. I could whip it out and piss on his leg and he wouldn't say a word. Nothing about him was Desert King material.

Preacher's need to control people was the only reason this weaselly punk was a probie.

He was Preacher's bitch.

"Didn't you grow up in the Bends?" I slapped a hard hand on his shoulder, all chummy and fake.

"Yeah." He turned to me, happy and smiling, but a little nervous. "When I was a kid, met Kenna there." He slapped her on the ass when she breezed by.

I gave her credit; she had one hell of a poker face.

"Bet you spent time with Wanda's boys while you were there too, right?" Ghost and Kenna were a few years younger than me. I'd went to school with the middle Haynes bastard.

The Bends was the collection of trailer parks and little shitholes that were tucked away in the bend of the dry riverbed. "Her youngest is about your age, isn't he? What's his name...Trent?"

I knew damn well that was the wrong name.

"Trey." Too late he realized his mistake and squirmed, the bar stool squeaking a little as he did. "I mean, we were in some of the same classes. Didn't hang out with him or nothing."

"Cool." I had him where I wanted him. He needed to squirm, and he needed to know that I *knew*.

His next move would give me ammunition to fire at Preacher. I caught Puck as he walked by... if anyone could keep Kenna out of that crossfire, it was him.

Nine

Riley

Driving myself was a strange feeling now. As a kid, I'd always felt this massive sense of freedom in my car, alone, with the radio blaring. That was nothing compared to riding on the back of Cam's bike, face tilted toward the sun as we tore through the desert.

Even thinking about it turned me on a little.

Dry Valley had made me a different person. I liked this version of me. I liked the excited tickle in my belly when I thought of riding out to Desert Lights on the back of Cam's bike flanked by the rest of the club.

Being with Cam made me feel important *and* sexy. The combination was exhilarating.

As I stepped out of the car, Puck was rifling around in his saddlebags. He smiled and tossed me a wave. I studied his bike for a minute. It was a similar make to Cam's but the crimson tank and fenders were covered in shadowy sketches of what I could only describe as fiery demons blazing across it, before being swallowed by smoke.

I was going to ask him if he sketched the art himself, but shouts echoed around the building from the back. The argument was loud and clear enough I could tell it was Kenna and most likely Ghost. On the heels of her visit a few days ago, I wasn't really surprised.

Puck heard it, too, but didn't seem surprised. But the big man moved fast, his long legs eating up the hard sandy earth and leaving me running to keep up.

By the time I rounded the corner, Ghost had Kenna by the shirt-front, screaming in her face. His movements were violent, his face beet red, veins popping out on his neck, spittle flying.

To her credit, my feisty friend was giving as good as she got. Struggling on the toes of her boots, clutching sparkling fairy wings in one hand, she pummeled his chest with her other. The only thing louder than Ghost was Kenna.

I might have been scared, but she wasn't.

Not seeing Puck and I, Ghost tossed her to the ground, where she hit and rolled like a child's baby doll. When he made like he was going to stomp on her, panic laced across me and propelled me forward.

"No!"

On the ground, Kenna rolled up onto her elbows, grinning and defiant. Then she spit at his face.

But Puck was already there, a solid wall of tattooed, pissed off muscle. He shoved the smaller man so hard, he fell to his knees and rolled on the ground a few times, similar to what Kenna had just done, only with much more force. The motion reminded me of a stunt man jumping off a moving train.

Puck had done it with minimal effort. I now understood why Cam had entrusted him to keep me safe. The man was a beast. He picked Ghost up by the throat and reared back with his fist.

Kenna was on her feet, zero fear. She jumped onto Puck's arm, hanging from it with all her weight, before he could throw the punch. He lowered that arm, but held Ghost up to eye level. The other man kicked his feet in the air, the size difference almost comical.

He gagged, face and head turning red, the color so dark it washed out the black tattoos of Ghost's skull.

"God damn it, Puck, *stop*! Jesus. Fuck!"

The way his eyes narrowed and his nostrils flared, he was about to put a serious hurting on Ghost. I wrapped an arm around Kenna, tried to tug her away, but she shrugged me off and went for Puck's other arm.

Then she gave up, placed both palms firmly on his chest. The moment she touched his chest, the big guy stopped moving completely.

"Please, Puck," she begged in a much softer voice.

He released Ghost onto the ground in a puddle of gasping, piss stained piece of shit. My anger was so deep, I felt like a piece of Cam was sliding out. Ghost coughed, spit, and rolled to his hands and knees.

"Go on, suck his dick, too, like the pass around you are," Ghost grumbled from the ground.

Puck surged forward again, one arm around Kenna to move her with him and keep her from falling.

"*Please*, leave it." This time, she lay her face against his chest.

He nodded once and glared over her head. "Get the fuck out of here until your sponsor calls you." His voice boomed with authority. "Or even she won't stop me from fucking you up."

Wiping the spit and dirt from his mouth, Ghost stumbled to his feet and took off in the other direction.

Kenna took a shaky breath. "Thank you."

Then she moved away, the same ball of restless energy she always was, and screwed her face up. "He thinks I sabotaged him and told you some shit." She avoided looking at me, like if she did, he'd know I knew something he didn't.

Puck was bewildered for a flash before he frowned. "Like what?"

"I don't know. Something about Cam." She snatched her wings from the ground and shoved her arms through them. "He's fucking crazy. Always worried about the damn patch vote."

"After this, he fucking should be," he snarled, talking more than I'd ever heard.

"You good?" He glanced at me, as if just realizing I was there.

I nodded, then rubbed a hand over my face. "I'm glad you were here."

Kenna ignored us both. Collecting belongings that had been scattered around in the sandy dirt. Her fairy wings winking in the sun.

"I'm going to need a ride to Desert Lights," she said to Puck as she shouldered her bag.

"You sure? It'll make what he said true," he said before holding the back door open for us.

"Yeah. Fuck him. If he's already telling everyone that, who gives a shit?"

"Won't that cause... more problems?" I knew enough to know riding on the back of someone's bike was a big deal.

"I don't give a shit," Kenna barked before taking my hand. "Let's go upstairs and get ready."

"You should probably consider a job as a matador or a lion tamer," I said as I followed her up the steps.

I wanted to ask her what she'd told Cam, what had made Ghost so angry. But this club business was a part of Cam I could never touch. Was I ready for that to be the rest of my life?

***

I was poured into incredibly short, glittery black shorts. They were Kenna's, which meant they stuck to me like a second skin, making my ass look bigger than it really was.

We'd paired that with a gauzy pink top with spaghetti straps that opened in the middle and flowed in the back. Kenna did my makeup, shimmering pinks and purples. I looked like a slutty Tinkerbell. But I drew the line at the fairy wings.

She wore them, though, over her sparkling tube top and skirt.

"You realize it's not Halloween, right?" Dylan sat on the edge of the bed I'd had sex with Cam in a few days ago, eying us with a hefty dose of speculation.

"It's a rave, Dylan." Kenna jerked a combat boot on over her neon purple fishnets. "Everyone will be dressed like this."

"And that's one reason I don't go." She curled her upper lip and turned to me. "It's not too late to back out. You can hang with me and dog sit for Jester."

Old Riley probably would have, but this me had gotten sucked in by Kenna's enthusiasm. Not to mention I didn't want to spend that much time away from Cam. But I was trying *not* to think about that.

"I'm kind of excited." I shrugged and found my shoes. I went for comfort and pulled on a pair of pink high-top Chucks I'd not worn in a long time. Mom had bought them for me, given them to me the day she'd told me about the cancer.

The pain from the loss swept over me, in a way it hadn't in weeks. I closed my eyes and thought of Cam downstairs. I pictured his face, chin jutted out and shoulders back in defiance, and I was stronger. My fingers didn't tremble as I tied the laces.

Kenna ducked out of the room, and I glanced at Dylan. "She and Ghost had a huge, ugly fight out back earlier." What I didn't say, was that I would go even if I didn't want to.

Dylan grimaced and softened. "Keep an eye on her. Kenna can be wild when she's upset."

"I will. She's riding with Puck." Their relationship was odd to me. A friendship, sure, but not like Dylan and Cam.

"Ooh boy, Ghost is going to lose his shit." Dylan snorted a laugh. "He hates Puck. He tries to hide it, but dude…"

"Puck choked the shit out of him when he acted like he was going to hurt Kenna out back." He'd practically emasculated the smaller man.

Dylan didn't even flinch at that statement. "Good, because he's a bitch."

"Why doesn't she just date Puck?"

"That's a lot to unpack, to be honest." Dylan plucked at a loose thread on the blanket. "Puck doesn't fuck around with anybody, not since all the shit with Jessica—his ex. I don't doubt Kenna would be interested, but I think it screwed him up so bad he focuses on his kid, his business, that sort of shit."

"Who?" Kenna came back, cutting to the mirror to smear on another layer of shiny lip-gloss.

"Puck." Dylan made an oops face at me and giggled a little.

"That man." Kenna dropped everything into a bag and glanced at me in the mirror. "His baby momma drama is enough to write a novel."

Dylan got off the bed and walked to the door, elbowing me an *I told you so* as she went. "You girls have fun. I've got to get things ready for the guys when they do shift change."

The girls had told me the Kings would switch off sometime in the morning, leaving a different crew to finish out the party. That meant coming home with Cam, which always left me excited.

I followed Kenna down the stairs, her wings bobbing in front of me. And for a moment. I was anxious. The clubhouse was all dark woods and leather, so were the guys... not glitter and pastels parties in the desert. Suddenly self-conscious about my outfit, I stopped a few stairs short and looked around.

You're being silly.

But half of me wanted to rush back upstairs to my jeans and tank.

Cam turned on his barstool. His eyes narrowed, his nostrils flared, and his tongue slid slowly over his lips. My heart pounded and my knees went weak.

He was on his feet and halfway across the room before I could make it down the final two steps. At the base of the stairs, he took my hand and spun me in front of him.

His low groan turned me on. "I can't wait until this shit is over." Then he pulled me back against his chest. "I'm going to rip off those tiny shorts and bend you over the closest thing I can find and fuck you until you can't breathe."

Oh yeah. I definitely wasn't going to change.

He spun me again, kissed me hard, then squeezed my ass with both hands. "I'm not going to be able to stop doing that," he muttered as he pulled away.

I liked it all and grinned. "Good."

"Let's get out of here." He tucked me under his arm.

The sun was almost down as we walked out, but the night air was warm.

I'd seen them run in a pack, but I'd never ridden with them like this. The sound was breathtaking. Literally, the rumble of all the Harleys reverberated in my chest and all the way down to my toes.

With this many, they rode two, sometimes three wide, on the long stretches of two-lane highway. Kenna rode on the back of Puck's bike, fairy wings surprisingly intact, her arms thrown out wide like the little hellion she was.

I tried it too, letting go of Cam and spreading my arms. The thrilling feeling caught somewhere between falling to my death and taking flight. Cam glanced at me in the mirror, his lips turning up in the slightest smile.

I wasn't ready to give this up just yet.

Ten

RILEY

Desert Lights was sensory overload. Music, lights, people all packed into a chunk of desert between two sets of foothills. The noise, rather than blasting out into the night, ricocheted back into the little valley.

When I turned to dance with Kenna, she barely noticed me.

Not for the first time or the hundredth, she was glancing down at her phone. We'd spent most of the night exploring each of the stages and booths, even having butterflies painted with body paint on our chests and necks. But Kenna was miles away for most of it.

The crowd was getting thicker now. Light shows and throbbing techno bass blared all around us.

And here she was still worried about her asshole boyfriend. It was too easy to get annoyed, think about finding Cam and taking him up on his promise. But I'd told Dylan I'd keep an eye on her.

"Now he's blaming me for not being here with him. Like, me being here is some huge embarrassment for him because I rode with Puck. Keeps calling me a slut. That fucker."

"You knew it was going to rattle him," I pointed out.

Her mischievous grin was quick and dangerous. "Right, right."

"Put him on ignore and let's have fun. I've never been to a rave, much less something like this." And it was huge. We were tucked behind several food booths, where it gave the illusion of quiet. Four stages with DJs were set up in a giant x-pattern, the booths all set up in the middle of that x. Food, drinks, first aid, and all manner of party vendors.

"Hey." She snagged my arm before I could walk off. The DJ shooting bubbles out over the crowd piqued my curiosity. "Ever done Molly?"

I blinked and she laughed.

"Ecstasy? The party drug?"

I hadn't. I'd never even smoked weed. "No."

"Want to?"

"Maybe." All around us there were lights and music and people. Most of which seemed to be partying on another plane of existence. Being with Cam was an experience, and I wanted to experience more things. Maybe be a little bad myself.

"Let's ask your boyfriend." She tugged me along behind her, stomping around in her fairy wings and combat boots.

"I don't need his permission." I scowled as I fell in step.

She laughed, high and bright. "He's the one with the drugs."

Somehow, I wasn't surprised.

Cam, in jeans and his leather cut, stood near one of the entrance gates. Jester and several others with him. He was laughing and at ease, which was sexy as hell. I enjoyed watching him, unaware that I was as we approached. In his element, he cut up with the guys around, but constantly had an eye on the crowd around him.

When he saw me, he peeled away with a grin and wrapped me up in his arms. He examined the body paint. "I'd like to see that without the rest of this shit on you."

He hooked a finger in the deep cut front of my shirt and pulled it back, glancing inside. Then was mock dejected when he saw my bra. "Damn."

But he kissed me like I was the hottest thing in the desert. Scorching all over me, one hand sliding down my ass and between my thighs, rubbing against my sex, openly marking his territory while he kissed me.

I pulled from the kiss, his hand massaging across my pussy through the shorts, with a mix of surprise and arousal. But I didn't push him away. He leaned close to my ear. "It's all mine."

When I chuckled, he nuzzled my neck. "You look so good, darlin', Every guy here is watching you."

I blushed and wiggled back a step. Kenna gestured at me to get on with it before rocking back and forth in her boots. Did I just ask? I'd never done drugs before, much less bought them.

"Do..." I looked around nervously and Cam screwed up his brow, both hands now clutching my ass. "...you have any Molly?"

His blond brows shut up in surprise. "For who?"

"Me and Kenna."

"Uh...huh..." he grunted, his eyes narrowing teasingly. "And if I happen to have some, what's in it for me?"

I wasn't a prude. I knew Molly was a club drug that might make me more sex forward, hornier. "Well, I don't have any cash on me." I teased and drummed my fingertips on his chest.

He took a long look at me, smacked my butt with one hand, then reached into his vest pocket.

It was my turn to be shocked. The bag in hand was filled with brightly colored tablets. I couldn't even comprehend that many, much less when I realized he wasn't the only one of the guys with them.

"It's safer when we provide the party," he said simply as he shook two out.

"You don't have a secret life as a small-town drug dealer?" I gasped.

"You know all my secrets, darlin'." His eyes were serious, but he shoved the bag into his pocket with his free hand, plucked a pill from his palm, and handed it to Kenna.

"How much do I owe you?" she asked, happily popping it into her mouth and swallowing dry.

"Riley's gonna pay me later." He grinned and held the other one out to me between his thumb and forefinger, so that I had to wrap my lips around both and suck it free before swallowing. I made a show of it, teasing him.

The fire that flashed in his eyes made me want to put my lips around other parts of him.

"And I expect to be paid in full." He slapped me on the ass one last time as I pranced away.

Desert Lights was amazing. I don't know what I'd expected, but Kenna and I danced from one stage to another, finding areas of parties where various social organizations, fraternities and the like had smaller parties happening within the big one.

It was late into the night when the chemicals kicked in. I found myself lost in the music as if it controlled my movements—not me. The musical marionette marked with flashing lights. Sights and sounds were brighter and louder, the music visceral.

Cam found me every so often when he made rounds around the event or got called to handle a disturbance near us. He'd pull me to him and kiss me, sometimes swaying with me while I ran my hands over him. He always pulled away before I could get more than a passing graze. It was like he knew if he stood there too long, I'd do more than touch.

At one point, I was dancing by myself under a flashing strobe light. Kenna flirted nearby with some young, college aged guys. Then Cam was there, his body hard, unyielding in front of me when he leaned down and claimed my mouth. No dancing, standing still as others undulated around us. His tongue enticed mine, slowly languishing against it, sliding back and forth. His hands slid up and down my sides, my ass, even between my thighs from behind like he'd done earlier.

It wasn't until I undulated against him, mimicking sex as best I could as I danced, that he untangled himself from me. I didn't need to hear the groan, because I watched his face contort with it.

I'd screw him right there in front of the crowd. I didn't care. I wanted him so much. I was desperate for his hands on me, his cock inside of me.

"Soon, baby." He nipped my ear before leaving me again.

With a huff, I went back to Kenna, wrenched her away from her boys. If they protested, I didn't care. Because the Kings were never far away. I could see them all over the place. Their dark leather cuts stood out starkly against the flashing lights, the patches glowing bright white in the black lights. It made me feel safe, protected, and able to enjoy a new experience my sheltered life hadn't allowed. Because the men in those leathers, the scary ones, the killers and drug dealers—they would protect me.

Kenna was a vibrant, sparkling ball of never-ending energy—Tinkerbell on speed. She tugged me to yet another spot broken off from the chaos of the main concert crowds. When she left me to make-out with two guys at once, I found a place to sit and found myself missing Cam. It was a weird, hippie vibe to sit on a small outcropping of rock in the desert and sway back and forth to the music as laser light shows flickering across my skin.

My grieving process started the day Mom was diagnosed. By the time she died, I was focused on survival. Alone in this large, loud crowd, I found a calming sense of quiet. I forgave and grieved for both my parents. Was sad for the one who'd given me everything she had and at peace with the one who gave me the life I had now.

"He's here!" Kenna's angry hiss was the only thing to pull me from my thoughts.

"Who?" Momentarily confused, I looked around for Cam—as I had most of the night.

"Ghost." She stamped her foot, a puff of dusty sand covering the toe of her boot. "Just when I'm having a good time, he's standing there, arms across his chest, glaring at me."

"Did you have your tongue down someone's throat?" Seemed like a good question, considering.

Instantly exasperated with me, she tossed up her hands, then slammed her balled fists onto her hips. "No," she said it with such force her wings bounced.

"Then screw him," I said, my tone as flippant as Cam's. After what I'd seen, Ghost wasn't nearly good enough for my friend.

That seemed to pacify her. But something in her demeanor settled weirdly on me. Maybe I was paranoid, maybe I was reading too much into it, but a steady pressure was building around Kenna. Like at any instant, she might combust.

We danced near the outskirts of another stage. At this point I couldn't tell the difference between stages or music or lights. Kenna moved from me to this cute, preppy guy and back again. He was shirtless, his hair mussed, and well on his way to drunk.

He was the type of guy I used to think was cute, the popular kid I'd probably have had a crush on if I'd never met Cam—who was so different. Better looking sure, but more—grittier, bolder, badder.

Damn.

Kenna grabbed me, laughing, dancing in a circle. Everything flowed together, the music, the lights, the glittering wings she wore that seemed like they moved all on their own. So much so that I didn't notice when Ghost circled back around to us.

He pushed the preppy kid off Kenna, knocking her to the ground for a second time.

"Whoa!" I shouted.

Kenna shot to her feet, punching Ghost square in the mouth. It was a slow-motion swing of her arm. He saw it coming, let it land, almost as if he liked the outburst. His head barely moved, but I'm pretty sure I heard the crack of skin over the music.

She was shouting, he was shouting. Everything around me throbbed and my head sounded like the inside of a vacuum and the punch ran on repeat several more times. I blinked, trying to center myself, make everything normal again—but it didn't happen.

Someone reached for me, a beefy hand with stubby fingers. I looked up to see Preacher sneering. His face was over animated, like the boogeyman in a low budget horror flick.

I took Kenna's hand and ran, threading us through the crowd. She still laughed, oblivious to my distress. With each step, the preppy guy, Ghost, and Preacher all seemed to disappear.

A fight broke out beside us near one stage. Bodies shoved against me, Kenna, all heat and sweat and angry violence. Strong hands plucked me out of it, Kenna too. Merc hovered over us, checking us for signs of injury, before mussing my hair with a wink.

I crouched to the ground, sucking in ragged breaths. It was too hot, too much was happening. Kenna collapsed beside me, no longer laughing. As Merc and several others broke up the fight, guys from other charters toted the offenders off.

Merc knelt in front of me. "You good?"

Yes. No. I wanted Cam. I panicked for a minute, unsure how to answer that, managed a nod.

He stood, shouted to someone, then knelt back seconds later with two bottles of water and handed them to us. "Drink this and come with me."

"Where?" Kenna barked. Puffed up like a pissed off rave pixie.

I took Merc's hand and ignored Kenna's resistance as I let him lead us through the crowd. I didn't follow blindly. Wherever Merc was taking us, Cam was there.

When I saw him standing in the middle of a crowd, it was like he was lit by a light that didn't exist. A glow exuded around him. A white, burning sort of confidence that made him sexier than any other man there.

I could eat him up.

The desert was too hot, too crowded. I wanted him alone. I was past the point of wanting this party to be over.

He looked up, saw me, and the corners of his mouth turned up slightly. I knew the glow didn't exist even as I saw the world currently in swirls of color. But the smile and swagger as he walked to me was absolutely real.

And was all mine.

A wave of people surged away from us to the crowd near a stage. Aggressive party goers, going at each other again. Instead of running away, the crowd pushed toward the violence. Bottles were thrown, fists flew, but pretty soon the fight was gobbled up by onlookers vying for a better view.

"Stay here!" Cam shouted as he ran by me, shoving me and Kenna into the first aid tent and tearing off toward the fight.

"Holy shit!" Kenna's mouth gaped, clutching my hand tightly now. Her tussle with Ghost, the little fight Merc rescued us from, had been nothing compared to this.

"That's crazy, bruh." Mr. Preppy Pants was back, face red as he gaped at the rolling crowd. "You ladies okay?"

We were fine, had been the entire time. But I didn't say that, couldn't find a reason to break through my high haze to waste words on him. He was nobody. Nothing.

The crush of dancers and fighters moved close to us, people darting across the desert to get away, climbing over fences and crashing into brush and tumbleweeds. Not to get away from the fight, from the party, but from the line of bikers in leather vests that waded off into the crowd dispatching the hooligans.

I looked frantically for mine while Kenna chatted up her new friend.

"Riley," Kenna was pulling at my hand. "This is too much; I'm getting out of here."

"What? Where?" I turned to Kenna as an EMT led in a young woman bleeding profusely from her nose.

"Anywhere but here. The fight, the noise, Ghost. I have to go." Preppy pants was leading her away.

"You don't even know these guys." I gave chase.

She screwed up her face. "I do. I graduated with Chad and Lance. Duh. It's just a house party. I'll catch a ride home after. Stick around"— she did a sexy little shimmy— "Enjoy your buzz and your man."

I didn't like it. The sick tug deep in my belly shouted that this was all wrong. There was a reason Dylan had asked me to keep an eye on her.

"Nuh uh. We stick together."

She was annoyed but shrugged a shoulder. "Fine, then come with us. But your boyfriend is going to be *big* mad that you left."

"He'll get over it."

The impatient way Preppy-Pants Chad huffed near the edge of the tent told me that my presence wasn't wanted.

Fuck that guy. I was definitely going now.

I fired off three texts immediately and turned on my location.

Worried about Kenna. She's going to some house party with people I don't know.

Going with her.

Come get me.

Eleven

CAM

I brushed the dust from the front of my cut and shoved the zip ties into the inner pocket. The adrenaline rush of the fight, of slinging people around, used to be more exciting. I'd be amped up for hours after. Since I'd had Riley, it wasn't. Touching her, tasting her, fucking her was a surge of adrenaline unlike any other.

But the exhilaration still ran white hot and electric. The rowdy crowd dissipated as Jester shoved the last of the would-be badasses into the back of a sheriff's van and slammed the door.

"Whoo!" He tossed his head back and shouted into the night air. He reminded me of a famous 80s' pro wrestler in yellow spandex.

If I told him that, he'd probably do it even more, so I kept my mouth shut.

Blowing the hair from my face, I looked around the area in front of the stage. The party was back in full swing, like we hadn't just broken up a mini-riot.

"I live for this shit, man." Jester smacked me on the shoulder.

I snorted. Wading off into a fight that had nothing to do with me wasn't as exciting as it had been when I was a teenager. Not since I'd beat a man to death. I blinked that memory away. "Save some for Fight Night."

"Oh, I got plenty." He winked.

"I bet you do, crazy fucking bastard." Ivan's voice cut in.

Ivan was president of the Reno charter and a longtime friend. About ten years older than me, could party harder than anyone I knew, and had a nasty right hook. The best part of these big events was that we called the other charters in. Shit like this was often the only time we got to hang out with some of these guys.

The strobing lights flickered off his bald head and reflected in his toothy smile. "And I know who I'm putting my money on." He snickered.

He was easier, more amiable than the last time I'd seen him. We all were. Archer's funeral hadn't been but a few weeks ago, and I could barely remember the man I'd been then. The man I'd been before Riley.

I whipped my head around to the first aid tent. I'd left her there, but she hadn't stayed in one spot for longer than a few minutes since she'd taken the molly. MDMA would do that.

It was worth it because damn, she was sexy as fuck dancing around in those tight ass little shorts and that wispy excuse for a top, rubbing against me, damn near molesting me in front of everyone.

She wasn't at the tent when I stuck my head in.

"They left with some young guy," the nurse there called to me over her shoulder.

Panic, jealousy, and anger seized my chest and brought me to a complete halt as I checked my phone. Sensing my shift in mood, Ivan doubled back to me, pulling Jester and a few of his guys with him.

If I'd been amped up before, I blew right past all control when I saw her texts—ten minutes too late.

On my way.

I snagged Merc as soon as I shot off my response. "Go find Ghost, tell him his ole lady went rogue and he needs to fix this shit. *Now.*" Puck had told me about the fight. If the little fucker wanted the patch, he had to earn it. So far, he hadn't.

"Problem?" Merc eyed me as I gestured across the crowd for Puck to come with me.

"She took mine with her."

Jester peeled off toward the security hub, Merc slipped into the crowd, and Ivan fell in step beside me.

"Get AP to bring the next shift out early," I shouted to Jester before he was out of earshot.

He tossed up two fingers, already on it.

I paused at the gate long enough to pull out a cigarette, light it, and take a drag. It didn't do shit to calm me down.

I wasn't waiting for anyone's permission to start toward my bike. I was back on the move again; Desert Lights be damned. The only thing that mattered was Riley. Anxiety ramped up in my chest, like a mob of angry crows pecking at my ribcage. Their clicking beaks drummed a steady beat, telling me to hurry.

Urgency, unlike anything I'd ever known, gripped me and shook those crows up to a frantic tempo.

I opened the GPS on my phone. A blinking little dot told me Riley had turned her location on, and I knew exactly where she was. *Thank fucking God.* When it finally stopped, I would be headed back to Dry Valley. Where we were Kings.

The bikes were parked in a sandy lot behind one of the stages. Several of Ivan's guys stood watch. I nodded to one of them before tossing my leg over my Harley and putting on the clear safety glasses.

Ivan himself was strapping on a shiny chrome helmet to my left. "Let's go get your girl, brother." He swung his hand in a circle in the air, and a couple of his guys left their group to jump on their bikes and ride with us.

I cranked mine and pulled from the row as Puck, Jester, and Dekes followed; the roar of their engines melding with mine.

After that, I didn't look back. My only focus was getting to that house as quickly as I could. Last I knew, it was a party house some fraternity from UNLV rented.

Bunch of preppy fuckers. If any of them had laid a finger on her, I'd burn the whole mother fucking thing to the ground with all their bitch asses inside.

The part of me I'd shelved, the one that had laid dormant in the days since I'd met Riley, was chomping at the chrome-coated bit. This is who I was. I was the bastard that would fuck their whole world up. Whatever I felt for Riley hadn't chained the monster. She'd set it free. For her, I didn't need a reason to kill. She *was* the reason.

My phone buzzed in my pocket. I plucked it out with my left hand and read the text, never taking my right from the throttle.

Hurry, they are taking our phones.

The hell they were. The beast inside me swallowed up all the flapping murder birds. It roared to life, spitting feathers, and so did my throttle.

I flew down familiar roads, passing cars, and blowing stop signs. My heartbeat in time with the broken yellow line in the middle of the pavement.

Behind me, everyone kept up.

It wasn't a possessive energy that flowed through me. This was deeper than that. Something I hadn't felt since that day I'd walked in and found my mom—eyes wide and vacant—blood leaking from the corner of her mouth.

The cold fear made me feel weak, the angry churn of guilt, weaker. I should never have let her run off tripping with Kenna. Big mistake. *My* mistake.

The beast inside me reacted, sucking away all those emotions until the only thing left was a violent swirl of rage.

I could kill a man like this. I already had.

Almost there, I slowed and a flexed my throttle hand to keep from trembling.

I was off my bike before anyone else parked. There were several young guys, kids barely, standing outside. They were fucked up. It was obvious by the way they swayed and how loud they talked.

They shut up when confronted with a pissed off Desert King, then scattered like the roaches they were.

"How hot we going in?" Ivan asked as he jogged up beside me.

"Burning this mother fucker down."

Twelve

Riley

"Look, it's not a big deal. We've all got futures to think about. Nobody here needs some random photo of him or her with a joint showing up on Veronica's Insta. You want to leave? Cool, grab your phone on the way out. No one is forcing you to stay." His name was Lance. He was bigger than the annoying Chad, more forceful, with wide set angry eyes.

There was another guy who flanked him. His entire round face was red with...what, I wasn't sure. But paired with the smushed nose, he looked like an angry pig. Maybe it was the Molly, but every one of them had facial features that seemed comical and exaggerated.

Blinking my eyes closed tight a few times, I shook away the unsettling feeling.

Cam and his crew were dangerous. You'd be more likely to see their faces on mugshots than college yearbooks. But Lance, Chad, and this crew presented a different kind of danger. This was the sort of party where years later, some bored housewife would be up late listening to a soothing narrator tell her how Kenna and Riley used to light up rooms.

Every inch of me screamed I should run, but I couldn't leave her. I'd never be able to live with that sort of guilt.

He's coming.

Lance was right. I could leave. In fact, I was pretty sure he wanted me to. The drugs made everything around me seem like each movement was swimming through flashing sound waves. The bass boomed out of speakers and flowed in incandescent greens all over Pig-face. Even still, I was probably the only woman here who saw what was really happening.

I wasn't leaving Kenna.

"Fine." I fired off one last text and tossed my phone into the basket. But not before I saw the *read* icon pop up next to it. I'd never had as much faith in a person as I did in Cam right then. He'd be here. Even Preacher couldn't stop him.

Kenna tugged on my hand, one of her fairy wings bent sideways, her eyes dilated, and her lipstick smudged. "Ry! The cute guy from the car?" She glanced back at a too pretty, fresh faced guy with Pig-Face and Lance in a little circle, talking. "His name is Kylar—such a stupid name." She giggled again. "But he went to school with me and Ghost. He hates him. Like serious, seething hatred. I'm gonna sneak off and make out with him. It'll get back to Ghost, piss him off epically."

My heart slammed against my ribcage and I went cold, uneasy. "I don't think that's a good idea."

Chad had joined Pig-Face's little pow-wow.

She screwed up her face, like she was debating what she was about to say, then relaxed with a resolute jut of her chin. "I get it. You aren't the same as me or Dylan. But we've been through shit. I got this; it'll be fine. Relax...it's a fucking party."

Her half-broken fairy wings bounced, never to take flight, all the way to Kylar and Lance. There were whispers between them, all snickering as they elbowed each other and gestured with their red plastic cups.

The sinking feeling in my stomach turned sour, sick, and dropped all the way down like putrid lead.

Chad and another guy followed Kylar and Kenna up the stairs.

My quick dash to get to her was so frantic, I stumbled on the bottom step. But I could only watch in helpless, sickening horror as the three guys entered a bedroom with Kenna and shut the door. I may not have grown up with bikers, but I knew predators and a bad situation when I saw them.

"Easy, there." Lance swooped in, helping me to my feet and tugging me off the bottom step. "Where ya going? Party's down here, darlin'."

Only one man called me that.

From Lance's drunken mouth it sounded sickening and made my skin crawl.

"I need to talk to my friend." I side stepped him and would have made it, had the Molly not made my legs shaky and unsteady. He grabbed my shoulders and shoved me back, before stepping in between me and that bedroom.

"Nah, we aren't going to do that. Let's get you a drink."

"Fuck off." I ran at him, shoving him in the stomach before jumping onto the bottom step. This time, I made it up a few stairs before the drugs left me unbalanced, clutching at the chipped and cracked handrail. Lance pounced, jerking me by a foot. My elbows cracked against the steps as I fell. The pain was jarring, running up my arms and ringing in my ears.

Then he jerked me to my feet by my neck.

I fought against him, flailing and slapping, until he squeezed my throat. The goofy, cheesy smile was gone. His eyes narrow and mean as he stole my breath. I flailed, imagining I looked much the same as Ghost when Puck had him.

Except no one was pulling on Lance's hands, forcing him to let go. I gagged, my vision blurring in and out.

"Your little bitch friend knows what she wants, so mind your fucking business."

He squeezed tighter and everything began to fade to black. The music was loud. The only thing I could make out was the loud bass that would have drowned out any scream I could make, even if he let go.

He must have realized what he was doing and dropped me to the floor, looming over me with nasty a sneer.

Lance was talking, but whatever he said was swallowed up by the racing hope of my heart. I'd felt this before. The walls were vibrating, the floor humming beneath my fingers. Not from the music, but in the way the clubhouse did when more than a handful of bikes pulled in.

Laughing, I struggled to my feet as Lance peered around, bewildered. No doubt he thought I was nuts.

One large bang at the front door, and the partying young people closest to the door scattered. Then another bang before the door flew off the hinges, slamming forward onto the ground narrowly missing a chubby guy double fisting beer.

I couldn't tell if he'd sloshed the beer on his crotch or pissed himself when confronted with more than six feet of muscled biker with tattoos all the way up his throat.

"Party's here!" Jester shouted in the doorway with such manic excitement everyone heard it, regardless of the noise. Black pistol in hand, he shot into the floor with a wood splintering boom. People screamed, guys hit the floor, several girls on the couch huddled together.

It must have seemed like something out of a horror film for them. Someone slid around him and jerked the cord out of the giant speakers. The bald guy I hadn't met but had been with Cam at Desert Lights.

"Nuh-uh, playboy, sit your punk ass down." Jester waved the gun at the buff football player type that was giving obvious thought to charging him.

And then there was Cam with a stream of leather clad Desert Kings filing in the door behind him.

"Where?" he asked me. Everything was so quiet now.

"Upstairs, room to the right." Puck, Merc, and several others charged up the steps.

"Hey, you can't just do that. Who the fuck do you think you are?" Lance tried to jump in the way, but Puck shoved him away with the same ease he'd tossed Ghost around with.

Lance stumbled down the last two stairs and fell on his ass at my feet. Oh, how the roles had changed.

I had the satisfaction of watching Cam hover over him, face hard and menacing. "We can and we fucking will." He pulled his pistol, pointing it right at Lance's face.

Funny, he pissed himself too. The rancid scent of urine made me cough.

"And you'll shut the fuck up. Got it?" Cam's eyes were wide and feral.

"Yeah." The douchebag wasn't so mean now.

Around the room, Jester was putting guys on their knees in the center. "Don't be scared ladies, I promise this time...we're the good guys."

When one girl grinned at him, he winked. "Unless you like it bad, sweetheart."

"Bottom of the house is clear." Dekes walked back into the room, leading a trio of frat boys in their undies and a pretty girl with braids from the back hallway. She looked—completely lost and afraid.

My heart thundered harder. How dare they, all of these bastards.

A brief glimpse of just how bad Jester could be flashed in his eyes when he saw the young woman. I turned away when he smashed one guy to the ground with one swing of the butt of the pistol.

Grunts, and the smash of skin on skin, echoed in the quiet space as he beat all three of them.

When I looked up, the bald biker was wrapping a throw blanket around the woman's shoulders before leading her to an empty place on the couch.

The tenderness seemed strange and out of place amidst such violence.

The scuffle upstairs grew louder more brutal with thumps and crashes as Lance frantically cast his eyes between where Cam held him at gunpoint and the top of the stairs.

Then Puck came thundering down, a bundle wrapped in a dark blanket in his arms.

"Kenna," I whispered.

"I'm getting her out of here," Puck stated simply to Cam before stalking out. No one else came downstairs. I didn't feel the slightest bit sorry for the assholes up there with Merc and the others. They deserved whatever they got.

Then Cam turned to me. "You okay?"

I brushed two fingertips across my throat, the skin still stung. "Yeah."

He tilted his head and looked closer, and my insides went cold.

Thirteen

Riley

I knew from the bar, and the peckerwoods, what would happen if I told him what Lance had done. Even as angry and scared as I was, I couldn't unleash that sort of violence—not on anyone. Not because I cared what happened to Lance. I didn't. What would it cost Cam to go to that dark place again?

The secret Cam had shared with me, what he was capable of, blazed in his blue eyes. I flicked a nervous glance to Lance, to make sure he understood, hoping the idiot would keep his big mouth shut.

That unconscious motion was all it took for Cam to *know*. He rounded on Lance, his eyes wild. "You put your fucking hands on my girl?"

Lance did a stumbling crabwalk backward and slammed against the wall. Nowhere to go.

Cam jerked him up by his shirtfront, leaving him struggling to balance on tiptoes. "You put fucking marks on mine?"

"I...I...di...didn't know, I'm sorry," he spit and sputtered, his voice breaking like he was going to cry. Around me, several of the frat boys were sniveling and in tears as Jester straightened, blowing hair out of his face, blood splattered on his shirt.

"Nah, shit stain, but you're about to be." There was emotion in Cam's voice, too. Rage threaded through each syllable until he no longer sounded like the man I knew.

I couldn't speak, couldn't move, as everything happened in slow motion. Cam released him and shoved the pistol in the holster at his side, under his vest.

Lance sneered at me, like he'd just won something. He was very wrong.

Cam jerked off his belt with a snap and looped it around Lance's neck before he could register the motion. Violence like this wasn't new to Cam. Violence against a man of equal measure wasn't new to him.

Cam didn't prey upon those he saw weaker. But this would be an easy fight.

With a flick of Cam's wrist, the leather snapped tight. Lance's cruel, overconfident smile vanished. Gone was the jerk that would have raped my friend, the man who would have hurt me.

He wasn't the one getting off on the power now.

There's always a *bigger* fish.

I stumbled to keep up with Cam as he dragged Lance out of the house. The other man was on his back, kicking, flailing and clutching at the belt where it cut off his oxygen. His face turning redder and redder as he bounced off the furniture, the floor, and the door frame. The asshole flopped down the steps behind Cam like a half dead carp.

One of the guys on his knees jumped up like he'd make a move to stop Cam.

But Jester was there, tossing him back down and punching him in the face twice. Then he shook a finger at the others and tsked. "Careful."

I watched the entire scene in a strange sort of awe. When Lance had grabbed me, choked me, he hadn't given a shit about Kenna or any of these women. He was one beer away from killing me. Why should I care about him?

Out in the night air, the watery daze I'd been in snapped to crystal clarity. Cam stopped on the lawn, put his foot on Lance's back, and pulled the belt impossibly tight, stretching Lance's neck back at such a painful level I glanced away to gather myself.

The gagging sounds Lance had made before changed to an awful squeaky sound. I forced myself to open my eyes and watch this—what? This was no fight.

It was torture.

Cam didn't release him until his face turned purple and his lips were blue. Lance rolled, unable to do anything but choke and puke.

"You're going to learn never to touch what belongs to me." Cam knelt in front of him and jerked his face up by the hair. "And all of your little friends are going to learn not to put their hands on a woman."

It was then I realized we had an audience. The frat guys Dekes had babysat had been marched out onto the grass. The girls were being shuffled by a still bloodied Jester to the far end of the porch. Even after everything he'd just done, he flirted with them.

Cam dropped Lance and turned to where Merc had walked out of the house, wiping blood from his knuckles. "Jester said they put all the girls' phones in a bag."

"Find Kenna and Riley's. Let the other girls have theirs back and make sure they get home."

As he said it, a cop car pulled into the drive, blue lights on but no sirens. Puck appeared from a chair in the shadows, cradling a barely conscious Kenna. He took the steps more gingerly than I thought the big man could and carried her to the cop car, laying her in the passenger's seat.

I recognized the cop as the deputy from Archer's funeral.

Cam glanced up at Jester as he strolled across the grass. Cam's face was cold and hard. "Fuck it. Drag these mother fuckers, then toss them in the river."

Chest heaving Cam practically bled anger. The emotion was so visceral I could see it in waves of red that ebbed and flowed and touched everything around him. He pushed his belt through the hoops of his jeans with deliberate motions, looking everywhere but at me. Like he was frightened of what I would see.

I should be scared, but I'd never been so turned on in all my life. Cameron Savage might have written Lance's death warrant tonight. There was a power in the fact that he'd kill for me. That power was so terrible and amazing I should run far away and never look back.

Never.

Wading through those waves of red, I went to him, and wrapped my arms about his middle. His pulse beat violently against my lips when I kissed the hollow at the base of his throat.

The night air blistered hot, white, and almost painfully through me. It was like only Cam could cool that fire. I pulled at my shirt and rubbed against him. I was safe. He'd come for me. Cam was here. I stretched to taste his lips. I sank into that kiss, melted against him, and soaked up all that red.

I wanted him, all of him, the violence and everything that came with what he felt for me.

The kiss was all heat and tongue; mine against his, him tipping my head back to take more. Then he broke away, shoving me a few inches from him, but clung to my hips.

"Baby," he whispered, breathless, sounding much the same way he did when he was inside me.

I whimpered a moan.

"Me too." And for the first time, the violence in his expression ebbed, replaced by something equally as hungry.

He dragged me by the hand to where Merc dumped the basket of phones on the ground and lit them up with his flashlight. Puck knelt and fished out Kenna's.

"Get yours," Cam commanded quietly.

I did, bending over and grabbing it with my free hand. Cam wasted no time tugging me toward his bike.

His leather clad back was solid and strong as I slid forward on the seat and all but climbed on top of him. Then the engine roared to life between my thighs. The vibration had never felt like that before. The reverberation was sexual and arousing as it hummed against me.

Cam tore out of the yard and onto the highway. My nipples were hard, tingling through the thin material of my bra as I raked them against the patches on the back of his cut. It was like I wore nothing and too much all at the same time.

I ran my hands down his chest, over his stomach, to his lap. My left hand caught on the hard ridge there, his cock straining against the denim. He was as aroused as I was.

Maybe it wasn't just the drugs making me this hot.

I stroked him there, up and down the length of his erection, and was rewarded when his cock jumped and the throttle lagged as his hand slipped.

This was a different type of power. Cam covered my hand with his left, slowed my strokes, and sped up on the bike. The wind, the light of the moon cascading over the desert, and the power of the engine humming between my legs only stoked my need.

I rolled my hips forward against the seat, the slightest of motions, pressing me against Cam's back and pulling the fabric tight across my slit. The vibration rolling through the fabric and across my clit. Over and over, faster and faster, until Cam gripped my hand tight, watching me in quick glances in the mirror by moonlight.

I came, an explosion of color and feeling as I clung to him. I cried out, clutching his cock with one hand and his hip with the other. I swore I could hear him growl as he slowed near an outcropping of short trees and bushes. He turned onto a long forgotten, eroded driveway. I nearly cheered when he stopped the bike and cut the engine.

Anywhere was good for me if it meant his hands were on me, his cock inside me.

Every detail was sharp and specific. It felt as if my entire body was covered in a soft, heady type of cotton—all arousal and desire.

The bushes had grown up and half hid an old, busted tractor. Several feet behind it was a steel trailer on blown out tires. Both were long forgotten by whoever had left them here.

Cam hopped off, picked me up, and sat me on the edge of the trailer. His blond hair was mussed, rebelling, and falling forward into his face, as reckless and wild as he was.

The urgency to touch him, to be touched *by* him, consumed me. I grabbed at his jeans and tugged at his belt.

"No," he panted, trembling. "Did you come on my bike?"

I nodded fast, kissed him hotly as he jerked my shorts and panties off, pulling me to the edge of the trailer and pushing my thighs apart.

Cam ripped his lips from mine and kissed my neck. His lips erasing the bruising that someone else had put there. "I need...to taste you," he said between kisses and then dropped to his knees, not giving me a change to protest.

Not that I wanted to.

His mouth was hot and wicked on my pussy. He kissed me there, with tongue and lips, and brushes of his teeth. Long. Slow. Deliberate. It felt...amazing and maddening all at once.

Whatever hesitation I'd had before about letting him go down on me was long gone. Pleasure shot up from my core. I leaned back on my elbows, face turned up to the night sky, and let that pleasure cover me in color and sensation.

Cam licked and sucked at me, running his tongue over every inch of my cunt. Like he was trying to drink up every inch of me. And all I wanted was to explode again. For all that pleasure, all that sensation, to combust for him. *Because* of him.

Every fiber of my being told me he could make that happen, knew at a primal level I just needed his mouth in one certain place.

I bucked against him, and Cam gripped my hips and held them to the trailer, keeping me still.

"Please." I shook with need, somehow more intense than I'd ever imagined possible.

Cam cast his blue eyes up at me. The moon was so bright I could plainly see the determined mischief glinting in them. He watched me writhe and beg.

"Say it, darlin'." He licked his lips with a slow flick of his tongue.

And I knew he tasted me.

"Make me come."

His response was to flick his hot, wet tongue over my clit. I bucked so hard against his hands he chuckled against my slit, his long fingers digging into the sides of my ass as he pulled me fully to his face.

Over and over, he drove me mad with that tongue. Was it the Molly? Or just him? I didn't know, but the onslaught of sensation was amazing. I bucked with it, ground my hips against him, and clutched at his hair.

I came again, crying out into the night with Cam making sexy, starving noises against my pussy.

When he stood, I was still wracked with tremors, all my muscles clutching tight. All the reds were gone now. Only my Cam remained, breathing hard and bathed in a pale white light, shadows dancing over his features. His anger abated.

He shrugged out of his cut and grabbed me up, my legs instinctively wrapping around his waist. Though his movements were aggressive and fast, he was gentle when he laid me on the ground on his leather, patch side up so that it never touched the ground.

"I can't wait, baby. Not another second."

Fourteen

CAM

"Then don't." Her sultry voice, thick with arousal, was so hot my cock jumped against my jeans.

"Fuck," I whispered, jerking my belt off as I looked down at her, legs spread open for me, thighs and everything in between wet and shining from her orgasm.

Riley was beautiful. She was everything.

My chest ached, rage ripped against my ribcage, desperate to hurt someone, anyone, who'd touched her. Kill anyone who even thought about it. But that emotion swirled with lust, blending until they become the same thing, making me the stuff of nightmares and Riley the only thing that could tame me.

I could taste her still, warm and earthy. I licked my lips and pushed my jeans down over my hips. No condom, because she was mine. *All mine.*

The slide of my cock inside her was faster than I'd wanted, leaving me little time to languish in her heat, to savor it like I had when I'd sucked her pretty little clit into my mouth.

The rocky sand below us dug into my denim clad knees. Not wanting to grate her skin, I lifted her legs and draped them over my shoulders. The position changed my angle inside her, tightening her pussy around me. I gasped, groaned and slid back out of her on an inhale until only the tip of my cock was wrapped in her tight folds. The heady scent of her slid through my lungs. God, it was like being consumed by her.

Nothing was better than this.

My slow stroke in earned a sweet, quiet moan from those full, pouty lips, and I came undone. The drugs made her insatiable. I didn't have that excuse. I was sober and still couldn't get enough. My arousal was all adrenaline and Riley.

I pushed her knees to her chest and lost myself.

Pouring every ounce of the violence that lingered inside me into each thrust, I turned that rage into pleasure, sensation, and something deeper I couldn't comprehend. Friction built, driving me closer and closer to release.

Beneath me, Riley's eyes were closed, and her pretty face upturned toward the moon. So fresh, so beautiful. Not made up and over done. Never. Not her. God, nothing in this world was sexier.

Sounds of sex were shouted into the night. Neither of us quiet, both of us groaning louder over the smack of skin on skin as I crashed into her, over and over.

She tightened impossibly around me, and I jerked. Her hands gripping tight to my hips as I growled out her name and exploded inside of her. I came, hot and hard. My hips pumping until every last drop of me was inside her. Until I was spent.

I didn't lay atop her. The ground was too rough. Instead, I rolled back on my heels, tossed my head back to the cool night air, and fought to catch my breath. I shook all over, not solely from the orgasm. The crash came as Harleys screamed through the night all around us.

Riley didn't know, couldn't, exactly what I was or what I'd just done. In the frat house, she'd looked at me with genuine fear in her eyes. Had she not done that, I'd have killed him right then.

This was the second time she stayed my hand—the first...Preacher.

I couldn't be held accountable for what happened now. The sleazy punk had signed his own death warrant.

When I glanced down at Riley, she watched, eyes cloudy with afterglow and ecstasy. "Can we do that again?"

I laughed and dropped a kiss to her lips before sliding out of her. "Once we get home, you're damn straight we can."

I cleaned us up with my shirt and dug a clean tee out of my saddlebags. She had perched on the edge of the trailer, feet swinging back and forth, by the time I finished.

"What will happen to them?"

I didn't bother to ask who, because I knew. Just like she knew I wouldn't answer that question. I shrugged my shoulders and pulled my vest back on. "Don't worry about it."

"And the girls? The other people there?"

That I could answer. "Are all on their way back home with a story to tell that no one is going to believe."

"That's how it works, huh?"

I bracketed her with a fist on either side of her hips and rested my forehead against hers. "This is what my life is, darlin'. Take it or leave it. It's who I am. Nobody touches you but me. Ever."

The corners of her mouth twisted ever so slightly. "As long as you make sure to touch me often."

Whatever I'd expected from Riley; it hadn't been that. She surprised me at every turn. She was too good to be true, damn sure too fucking good for me.

And if I had my way, she'd never figure that out.

The jolt of realization snatched my breath so fast I had to spin away from her and march toward my bike.

I was falling for her. Not even a screaming ride through the desert could chase that fact away. I collected myself and called back to her. "Let's go."

On the ride home, we were both quiet. Me processing whatever it was that I was feeling. Her coming off the MDMA. The sun was rising in the east, casting a pale glow over Dry Valley as I rolled home. I didn't get on the throttle, didn't rush. No need to.

She was safe with me. I knew that from the warmth of her hand on my middle that I covered with mine on the straightaways.

We were off the bike and walking into Archer's house when my phone buzzed with a text from Preacher.

Chapel. Noon. Full table.

I snorted, already knowing what it was about and didn't care. I'd made an executive call; I'd take the heat for it after I had a few hours in bed with Riley.

She downed a bottle of water, curled on the bed in the room that used to be mine, and was asleep before I could shuck my cut. Hair was tangled all over her head, that damn fairy shirt long gone, boots by the bed, and her hand stamp from the party was smeared across her face. She'd fallen into bed completely naked. Such a delightfully delicious mess that my cock twitched.

And she was the most beautiful creature I'd ever seen. I had zero guilt; the little bitch that choked her wouldn't survive the night.

***

Merc and Puck waited on me outside the clubhouse. The only other bikes in the lot were table members. With Desert Lights winding down out in the desert, the place was dead. I wasn't in the mood to deal with anyone, anyway.

Leaving Riley's bed to deal with Preacher's bullshit pissed me off.

"You ready for this?" Merc lifted his brow and looked about as tired as I felt.

"Fuck him." I spat, jerking the door open as I stalked past both of them.

Was I ready? Hell yes, I was. This shit had been building for weeks.

Puck grunted and walked with me. Jester leaned against the pool table, scrolling through his phone. In a world where I didn't know who to trust, this group was the closest thing to security I had.

"We good?" I asked, needing to know after what happened.

"Ain't nobody trying that shit again." Jester grinned, chest out a bit. "It was a nice ride through the desert."

"Cactus rash." Merc chuckled.

"Already made the news." Puck nodded to a flat screen television hanging in the corner. "Haynes and the others have it handled."

I didn't even bother to read the headlines. What was done was done.

The older generation, paired with Preacher's goon Paul, were already around the table. Dekes first real meeting, he was kick backed sipping a cup of coffee, ready for the big show. Goofy fucker got off on this bullshit drama.

"We all here?" Preacher scooted his seat back with a screech, making room for his gut, and leaned forward on his elbows. "What the fuck was that last night?"

I held my hand up, silencing Dekes before he could say anything. "That was taking care of ours. What the fuck do you think it was?"

"Your order?" His eyes narrowed, ready to fight.

"They were gang raping your prospect's ole lady. While another one choked Archer's fucking daughter—my ole lady. You better be fucking glad I didn't shoot that mother fucker where he stood, in front of all those witnesses."

"Getting the girls out, fine." But he was building up to the big show.

I made a tight fist under the table.

"Ordering a hit on four college punks brings too fucking much heat, and you know. Neither of those bitches are worth that."

My jaw snapped tight, and I spoke through gritted teeth. Across the table, Merc straightened—knowing what came next.

"It's what Archer would have done."

"You ain't him, and you don't get to make those choices!" Preacher boomed, fuming and stood.

I jumped to my feet, the chair falling behind me, and slapped the patch on my chest. "The second I put this on, I do. You weren't there. I made the call."

"And dragged in another charter, which you know damn well we don't fucking do. You're hot headed and rash, like that shit with the peckerwoods. You aren't thinking clearly. Bowman's kid is clouding your judgment."

"Fuck you, Preach. I can see just fine." Then I grinned. "The peckerwoods? You really want to go there with me?"

"What are you saying, son?" Preacher growled low and leaned forward on his knuckles like the goddamned gorilla he thought he was.

"Enough." AP's smooth voice cut through Preacher's bullshit. "Ivan went on his own. Brought his own guys, because that's what the Kings are about. We protect what's ours and have each other's backs."

"Or did you forget that?" I spat at Preacher.

There was a flash of something in his eyes and at that moment, I *knew*. I didn't need proof. That quick glimpse of guilt was enough to know he'd killed Archer. If he hadn't pulled the trigger, he might as well have.

But why?

I was too mad to give a shit right then. "You want this patch, old man? Want to take skin off me for that order? Try it. Vote on it. Now. Because that's the only way you'll fucking get either."

He took inventory of the room, and if he'd thought he had a chance in hell, he'd have called the vote. He didn't. "If this blows back on us, I sure the fuck will."

"None of the girls at the party or their families will talk. Hayes County Sheriff's Office made sure to spin us as the good guys. A few will say they saw the guys leave together in that car. That's all they know, that's all that matters." This from Merc, straight to the point. We had that sort of pull, always had in the county. Preacher knew that.

He smacked the gavel on the table and stormed out without a word to me or anyone else. Paul and Drop Top followed.

Anger still thrummed and vibrated inside me as I picked up my chair with shaking fingers.

"You good?" AP had come around the table, gesturing to everyone else to file out.

"No." There was no reason to lie; he knew me too well.

"I'm going to send Merc to Archer's."

"I've got Riley covered." After last night, I hated having her out of my sight for even a minute. Already I was antsy to get out of here, to get to her.

"It ain't her I'm worried about." He squeezed my shoulder once and strolled from the room.

I wasn't planning on doing anything stupid, not when I had Riley. She was my only tether to any sort of self-control.

Fifteen

RILEY

Cam didn't argue with me when I texted him that I was leaving. I think he understood my need to see Kenna after last night. It wasn't until I was punching in the address Dylan had given me that the trepidation sank in.

Last night had been...unlike anything I'd ever experienced. Thinking back to the party and the violence there, the entire scene rolled around until I couldn't breathe. Like I was reliving it all over. Then I thought of Cam, the slayer of my demons, and I sucked in a deep breath and felt instantly steadier.

If I broke the frat house into two separate events, the Kings' involvement was by far the more violent one. And yet, they weren't the bad guys. They'd saved us.

I knew the law enough to know that he could end up in prison. My biggest fear now was him paying that cost. Lance, the others, they'd have hurt more than just us. Men like that were the real monsters.

They'd never change. They'd just grow more adept at hiding their true colors.

Fuck that.

Dylan's Jeep was already in the gravel drive. I parked behind it and walked up to the porch. There was a shop to the left, bits and pieces of scrap metal and half-built bikes littered the yard. This felt like a biker lived here, for sure.

The man who opened the door was vaguely familiar. His smile was warm, curving the ends of his salt and pepper mustache.

"Hi, Riley." He pulled the door open and gestured me inside. He was tall and thin, and his eyes crinkled when he smiled. "I'm David. We met briefly at the funeral."

One in the sea of faces I played court to in front of Archer's casket.

"I don't get down to the clubhouse much anymore. Hadn't had much of a chance to talk with you. Got some stories about your dad, if you ever want to hear them."

He stopped me in the hallway, his face turning solemn. "They're in Kenna's room. That girl, she's never had many people look out for her. What you did last night is huge to me. Thank you, and I owe you."

"You don't owe me anything." Uncomfortable with the praise, I looked down at the scuffed toes of my Converse.

"All the same." He dipped his head and wandered off in the opposite direction, followed by the telltale creak of a screen door closing.

I stood in Kenna's doorway and smile weakly.

Dylan sat in a chair near the window. Kenna was curled on her side on the bed, on top of the covers, with her knees pulled to her chest. She'd showered, her damp hair pulled back from her face, and she was dressed in cartoon pajama pants and an oversized Desert Kings t-shirt.

She jumped up when she saw me. I had a second to brace myself before she threw herself around me in a fierce hug. Whatever trepidation

I'd had about coming here vanished with her embrace. She was okay, we were okay. Nothing else mattered.

"I'm so sorry," she said, her voice muffled against my shoulder. "I never should have dragged you into that."

The relief that she was still...Kenna made me lighter. "Never apologize for that again. I'm glad I was there."

She pulled away and the three of us were silent for a while. Dylan, reclined in her chair, had no doubt already lectured Kenna on where she went wrong.

I didn't need to pile on, so I didn't.

This room was different from the rest of the house. On my way in I'd seen dark panels, the occasional motorcycle photo, Desert Kings memorabilia, and a random assortment of masculine stuff. It was sort of suffocating, in a way.

Kenna's room was neat, the walls a bright cream color, with feminine landscape prints and posters from her youth dotting the walls. There was familiarity here. So many things I'd put in storage were similar. This had been her childhood bedroom. Being here made me nostalgic.

The silence grew thick, and we needed a change of subject. "How long have you lived here?"

Dylan was already tapping her foot restlessly and flicked on the television before Kenna could answer.

"Since I was about twelve? Sixth grade, I think." She sat on her bed and waved for me to join her. "My mom was dating David, and we moved in. But that didn't last long. She got arrested and sent away. Instead of sending me to a foster home, David let me stay. I've been here ever since."

Another story about how the Desert Kings had served as someone's surrogate family softened what Cam had done. Something else I saw in shades of gray.

The truth would never be black and white for me again.

Maybe I was more like Archer than Mom. She'd seen the life he lived as something firmly in the black. Dark, dangerous, the sort of thing she'd tried to scare me away from. From what I could tell, Archer had seen a way to make his life count.

"You okay?" I stopped ignoring the Big Ugly Thing that hung between us and sat on the bed beside her.

"They didn't rape her." Dylan said, relaxing against the chair and squeezing her eyes closed tightly. "But they would have."

Kenna rested her head on my shoulder. "You got them there, just in time. You saved me."

I took her hand and squeezed it. "We stick together." The Desert Kings' surrogate family was mine now, too.

"Check this out." Dylan straightened, turning the volume up on the television.

"Hayes County Sheriffs have identified the four men killed in a single car accident last night. Deputies say it was clear that drugs or alcohol played a role and that the single car drove off into the Dry Valley River..." The newscaster's voice trailed off as four images appeared on the screen.

"River?" Everything I'd seen was desert, dry and begging for rain.

Dylan glanced up. "Not really. It's a big ass dry river bed, floods when it rains and runs out of the county."

Chad was the second in the row. Then Lance, bordered by their two cronies, including Pig Face.

I sucked in a breath, the room twenty degrees colder than it had been. Cam's voice filled my ears.

"Drag his ass."

The room slowly spun as a busted red sports car flipped over on its side, and covered in yellow crime scene tape, filled the screen. I'd known. But seeing it made it harder to ignore. Cam might not have killed them—but he was the reason they died.

He'd done that for me.

And I was bad enough to be proud of that without feeling a single ounce of shame. They'd never hurt another woman again.

"Damn," Kenna breathed the word, almost reverently.

"Turn it off." I said then turned to Kenna and spoke tenderly. "It's up to every man to make choices. They made bad ones. Wasn't your fault."

"I needed to see it. But now we don't talk about it again." Dylan's voice broke a little. "We don't want to risk saying the wrong thing to the wrong person."

My fight with Cam at The Black Cat came full circle, I understood now why he'd been so upset with me.

"Karma rides a Harley," my whisper resounded in the quiet of the small bedroom.

"The secrets are easier to keep, the longer you stay in Dry Valley," Dylan said from her chair.

She wasn't wrong, not even a little. It seemed with every step I took, I held onto more of them. Too many people covered up too much here. Now I was one of them.

I thought of Cam, what he'd done when his mother died. That secret killed whatever innocence he had left. Made him into the man that did—the mangled car flashed in my mind—things like that.

He'd done it for me. Something else that shackled him to the club.

Sixteen

CAM

Riley was with Kenna. Instead of heading toward Archer's to hang out alone, I turned toward the winding stretch of highway that slipped through the edge of the county and butted up against a state park.

Here the desert gave way to rolling hills and bright, painted rock formations. It was like riding through an alien planet. I had too much going on, too much to think about. I needed to slow it down, make sense of shit.

Preacher had killed Archer.

He'd tried, twice, to intimidate Riley.

He wanted my patch.

And he was fucking around with my godmother.

"Shit."

I turned the bike, kicked it into gear, and headed toward Ro's place. She'd be off, probably asleep. But something in my gut had soured. There hadn't been many people in my young life I trusted, looked forward to seeing, or who made me feel loved. Ro was one of the only ones.

I wouldn't have this life if not for her and Archer.

We'd seen her at the diner. She could have easily overheard Riley and me talking. I hadn't thought of it before, because I didn't want it to be true. The past few days had proved that the only two people Riley and I could trust fully were each other.

Ro had broken my heart. Now I needed to hear her say it. Before I cut her out of my life, I had to know.

I pulled down the familiar gravel drive. A few sturdy trees had tried to grow here, most likely from Ro's attentions. Her cactus garden flourished in front of the deck I'd helped build a few years ago.

A mixture of betrayal and hurt swamped me. It was like being a kid all over again. I hated the vulnerability. Climbing off the bike, my stomach folded in on itself and bile rushed up the back of my throat.

One look at Ro, standing on her tidy porch, arms wrapped around herself, and I had all the answers I needed. She thought her relationship with Preacher was real. I was too damn mad for pity.

"Want to come in?" She was hesitant, afraid even.

Scared of me. That was fucked up. I wanted to throttle Preacher just for that. No matter how pissed off or hurt I was, I'd never lay a finger on Ro. She'd raised me, loved me, and just like Archer, got sucked into Preacher's manipulations.

"Nah, I won't be here long."

She recoiled with a sort of sadness, looking twenty years older than how I saw her in my mind. Would Mom have looked like this? A healthy woman in her mid-forties, with lines showing around her eyes and at her neck?

I hadn't thought much about Mom since Riley came into my life. She'd distorted all the painful things, sandblasted them until even the color of the blood was gone.

But when I did now, it was like being dropped off in front of this place by child services all over again. Hell, her robe looked old enough it could have been the one Ro was wearing that night.

"I'm sorry, Cameron, I should have told you." Tears welled in her eyes. She wiped them away with the back of a trembling hand. "And I'm so sorry you lost him, so sorry for all the bad things—"

"Stop." I rubbed a hand across my mouth and chin, then shoved it in my front pocket. "I don't want to hear any of that bullshit." Then I pounced. "Why Preacher?"

She balked, then her face went hard. "I'm allowed to have a personal life."

"You could have picked any man in the fucking state. Why him?"

"Do you not want me to be happy, Cam? Isn't he allowed to have a life, too?"

"I don't give a fuck about what he does outside of the club." I laughed without humor.

"Seems like you do." She made a point, but I was past caring.

"I thought, with how close you've grown to Riley, maybe you could understand." Her expression slipped back to sad.

"That's not the same. And what you know of that is a distorted version he fed you."

"He said you'd say that."

"No shit. Preacher is a manipulative fuck. He's using you to get to me."

"He said you'd say that, too."

Of course he did. I rolled my eyes and turned out toward those two trees again, to keep from losing my shit on her.

The wood of the porch creaked as she stepped closer and leaned against the railing. "Whatever is going on between you and Preacher, he really wants what's best for you, for the Kings."

"That's a mother fucking lie." This time when I faced her, I was beyond angry. My rage must've shown because she recoiled like she'd been shot. "When you told him we'd been at the lawyer, he took that information and showed up at Archer's trying to intimidate Riley, scare her. Then tried to take my patch this morning. And you think he cares about *me*?"

She didn't correct me, instead she dropped her head in defeat, admitting with that one move that she had told him.

The closest thing to a mother I'd ever had, even when Mom was alive, had betrayed me. I stepped onto the bottom step and let all my anger leak out. "The biggest joke is you believing he cares about you. That a woman as smart as you can't see what a piece of shit he is. And when he's done hurting me through you, he's going to toss you to the side like desert roadkill."

"You should be happy for me." Crying now, she closed her eyes, not daring to look me in mine.

A memory of Mom surged forward; one Riley hadn't scrubbed away. Each time I railed against whatever new junkie guy she'd brought home, she'd turn on me. Her desire to be wanted, or whatever the fuck it was, had cost me a childhood.

"You sound just like her."

"Your mom—"

"Said the exact fucking thing each time she found someone new."

Ro shook her head no, tears falling freely. "This isn't the same, Cameron."

"Funny." I climbed on my bike, unable to watch her cry. "The betrayal I feel, this pain in my gut? It's exactly the fucking same."

"Cam..."

I fired up the engine and took off before I said something even more damaging.

Preacher would drop her as soon as he realized he couldn't use her to get to me. She couldn't say I didn't warn her.

Riley was still at Kenna's when I got back to the house. I sat at the table under the carport, kicked my feet up, and rolled a blunt from the bag in my pocket.

"God damn it, Archer." I cursed out loud. He'd put me in a hell of a place. Everyone I cared about was circling the drain.

Fuck.

I was still sitting there, smoking, when the sound of Harleys approaching broke into my thoughts. Merc's I could tell from sound alone, and someone else.

Several seconds later he coasted into my driveway, Puck right behind him.

"Hear him out," Merc said, as he hopped off the bike. He was amped up; out of nowhere, suddenly bursting with energy and emotion. He'd been that way since he'd come back from deployment. Calm and unshakeable, until he wasn't. Then it would take him days to wear back down. He'd be ready for a fight the rest of the fucking week.

Puck got off slower. His face was solemn, like something really bothered him.

"What's up, brother?" I passed the blunt to Merc, who hovered as Puck collapsed into the chair across from me.

"It's been a long-ass twenty-four hours." Puck soothed a hand over his beard.

Amen to that. "How's Kenna?"

"She was out of it when I saw her. But Dylan says she's better today, up and about and whole."

I didn't want to know how bad it was, didn't need to, and wasn't planning on asking.

"We got there just in time," Merc told me, anyway, as he passed the blunt to Puck.

"Any blowback to get Preacher all wound up again?" I'd smoked nearly half the fucking thing by myself and didn't feel shit.

"It's all over the news." Merc nodded to my phone. "Regular sort of coverage, not a whisper of us."

It only took a few quick swipes of my finger to see the report. Four dead. Car crash. All fairly anti-climatic. I felt no guilt. One of them had put his hands on Riley. I'd have killed him right there in front of her, but I hadn't wanted her to see that.

The rest of them, well, they wouldn't be gang raping anyone ever again.

I was tired down to my bones, regardless.

"How's Riley?" Puck asked on a short cough.

"She's good."

"About all of this." Puck took another contemplative drag and passed the blunt back to me. "As we were leaving Desert Lights, I ran into Preach and Ghost. Told Preach what was going on. He shrugged it off, said it wasn't a club problem."

He leaned forward, lips tight. "Then he brought it up sideways at Chapel this morning. But brother...I don't like the way this is playing out. Letting the peckerwoods off scot-free, this shit, his sudden desire to have that little fuck patched in, but threatens to rip yours? Something's off."

Then he looked from Merc, unsure, and back to me. "One of my tattoo artists fucks around with one of Garza's guys. Said they were asking her about Preacher."

"Remember what we talked about?" Merc grunted.

Loyalty. Last night, and this morning, had showed me which guys would follow me into battle. Even if it was against Preacher.

"If the cartel is looking for him, that explains a lot." The man had vices. He and Archer had argued about them a lot.

"You've got the votes to take his place," Puck mused.

"I don't want it." Fuck that, no way in hell. Not since I'd met Riley. I was finding better things to consume my life than the club.

Which was a crazy fucking thing to think about.

Unless she left, then I'd have nothing. My heart stuttered in my chest, and my lungs pulled tight.

"You're the only one the younger guys would back." Merc paced near the table, speaking over his shoulder. Restless.

"We'd all back your dad." Neither of them could argue that. "But we don't need to go that far. Not yet." Not until I figured some shit out.

I couldn't tell them all my suspicions, not yet.

"What did you say to Ghost?" Puck changed the subject. He shifted in his seat. "I beat his ass."

"I rattled his cage. Nothing important."

This time Puck grunted.

"Shits going to get real at some point," I said, because I had to give him something. "Keep your eyes open, especially where he's concerned."

"You think it's all connected? Archer dying, the peckerwoods?" Puck stopped short of saying Preacher's name.

"Archer didn't have a god-damned reason to off himself." Merc's words were sharp, matter of fact.

I held my tongue. Let him draw his own conclusion.

"Jesus." Puck tugged on his beard with a shake of his head. Then he stood, stalked toward the edge of the carport and stared at nothing.

"If half the table went rogue, it would make him look weak. Force him to do something stupid...out himself," Puck said.

"You got any ideas?" I mused.

Merc turned to me, grinning. "I might have a few."

Seventeen

RILEY

Cam wasn't alone when I pulled into the driveway. Puck and Merc were there as well, and they all sat around the table beneath the carport. It was like Cam was holding court.

Having not seen the other two since last night, panic climbed up the back of my throat. I wasn't in that frat house anymore, Kenna was safe, and yet... I closed my eyes, took a breath, and climbed from the car.

I'd have to face them all at some point.

"Hey guys." I gave a short wave as I rounded the corner, beelined for Cam, and bent to kiss his lips.

Like he could read the nervous energy bouncing off me, he caught the back of my head, and held my mouth to his, kissing me low and slow. When he let go, his blue gaze was bright despite his eyes being bloodshot, and he searched my face. I knew what he was looking for.

He'd felt my fear and thought he was the cause.

He was wrong. Giving his hand a squeeze, I willed him to understand I was a part of this now. *His.* And the ride over had given me a clear goal, a path for what I wanted for the rest of my life to be.

"How was she?" Puck asked from behind me.

"Honestly, really good. I was surprised." I turned to him, perching, for a moment, on Cam's right knee.

His arm slid around me, pulling me back against his lap. The little tingle of pleasure when he did was something I'd never get used to.

Puck seemed relieved, relaxing visibly.

"She was getting her stuff ready to be at your house in the morning, to babysit or something."

He straightened. "The fuck? No." Then he plucked his phone out and dialed. His knuckles were busted and scabbed, like he'd been in a fight. Because he had. "Kenna, what the hell?" He growled into the phone and stood, pacing under the carport while talking softly.

The sheer size of Puck was intimidating, but I'd seen him cradle Kenna like she was the most precious thing in the world. Maybe he *was* the best of them. Or would be, were it not for Cam. I patted his arm. "I think I'm going to look through some more of Archer's stuff and chill for a while."

He kissed my hair and slid a hand across my thigh. "Cool. I won't be long."

With that, I went inside.

I had so many things I wanted to tell him, needed to tell him. But not until we were alone. Was this what falling in love felt like? Rushing head long into lust, then coming to an abrupt halt because suddenly the feelings were too big to hurdle?

To busy myself, I went through Archer's books. I picked some out that looked particularly well loved. I was beginning to think he spent as much time reading as he did riding.

The guys' lowered voices and occasional laughter put me at ease. That lonely, dark place in my chest that had grown when Mom got sick was gone now. Whatever I'd searched for, I'd found here with Cam and the Kings.

They were my family now. If he'd have me. And I'd protect them all with the fierceness surging through me at the thought of losing any of this.

With a heave, I lifted one box of political thrillers and carried it to the kitchen table, stopping long enough to peek out the window at Cam and the guys. There was an easiness, almost an innocence, here that had been missing last night. Two halves of the same coin. Flip it and find the violence, the danger.

But for now, the beast that was the Desert Kings MC slept. Was it like this for my father? I could almost picture it. Him in the leather cut, charging in with the entire MC at his back. Then kicked back in the well-loved recliner, cowboy novel in hand.

In the kitchen, I ran my fingers across the cracked spines. One in particular caught my attention: *The Walking Drum*. I plucked it from the box, padded back to the living room, and curled into that recliner with the book.

I wasn't sure what I was looking for, maybe a way to feel close to Archer, to thank him for what he'd left behind for me. The money had brought me here, but that wasn't what I'd needed the most. Cam was.

When I opened the book, a plastic keycard emblazoned with the logo of a storage facility and the numbers *three-three-two* fell out and into my lap.

The logo was familiar. I'd seen it before.

"What are you reading?" Cam asked from the kitchen, his voice almost swallowed up by the roar of the two Harleys pulling from the driveway.

I palmed the keycard and shrugged. "One of his books. Looks like he'd read it more than once."

"Probably. He read a lot." He scratched the back of his neck and twitched a little, like maybe he was nervous.

I'd noticed him do that a few times. It was cute.

"What's up?" I closed the book, letting the keycard slip back inside like a bookmark.

"Outside, you looked like there was something you needed to say."

And there were...so many things.

I stood and went to him, placing the book on the coffee table as I did. "You're afraid I'm going to run, aren't you?"

He nuzzled against my hands as I cradled his face. His cheeks were rough, like he needed to shave, but he smelled clean and wild, in a way that made me want to crawl all over him.

"Maybe," he whispered, as if afraid to hear it.

"Never." I kissed him, sliding my tongue against his until my entire body warmed, and I pressed against him, dropping my hands to his shoulders.

He pulled away after a minute. "Don't say that."

His eyes were serious, sad even.

"I mean it. I've been thinking and...I belong here, Cam. With you. I think he knew that."

I wasn't prepared for the way he jerked away from me, laughing without humor as he turned around. "I killed them, you know that, right?"

"No. You were with me."

He snorted and turned. "Doesn't matter, because I would have. I *have*. Want me to tell you what we did to them? Spell it out for you? Think my mom's asshole boyfriend is the only one? No, baby, he was the first."

I steadied myself, his anger stinging more than his words. I knew who he was. I'd already damned myself right along with him. I loved him. This was who we were.

"Last night you were with me." I didn't go to him, even though I wanted to. I didn't address the rest of what he said, because it didn't matter. "And that's what you'll tell anyone who asks. That's all I'll hear you say from here on out. Whatever happened to protect people you care about. It was deserved and it's over. *Finished*." There was a sternness in my tone I hadn't used in months, hadn't needed to.

"You are..." He stared at me with what I could only describe as a touch of awe.

"Archer's daughter. And right now, Cam, I really need to go for a ride."

"Yeah." He rustled in his pocket, pulled out one set of keys, rolled them around in his hand, and shoved them back in, before pulling out his. "It's cool. I'm going to grab you a hoodie."

"I have some—"

His grin was pure sex. "Yeah, but I like you in mine."

***

Wrapped around Cam, speeding through the desert, was when I felt the most alive.

He turned off the highway toward the mountains that bordered Dry Valley. The late evening sun had turned the buttes and hills gorgeous shades of purple and red. Cam shifted seamlessly through his gears until we were flying through those mountains.

These roads were two-lane, with big sweeping curves that seemed to stretch out forever. I'd been warm at first, but as we climbed, I became thankful for his Desert Kings hoodie.

Beneath his cut, Cam wore one that matched.

As we descended, he made a left, brought us around the foot of the mountain, and pointed us back toward Dry Valley just as darkness settled over the desert. The ride lasted most of the evening, as if he knew exactly what I'd needed.

Maybe he'd needed it too.

When we stopped for gas, I bumped into a young woman coming from inside the store. She was beautiful, though her hair was pulled back from her face and she wore no makeup.

"I'm sorry." Her voice held a slight accent, familiar but not something I could place.

Then her smile brightened when she saw Cam walk up behind me. I glanced back as he winked at her. But she continued on, sauntering out toward a dark sedan.

"I've seen her before," I said, shoving my hands in the hoodie pocket and contemplating the candy aisle.

"At the club, one of Val's girls, remember?" He picked out a pack of Skittles.

I did, I'd seen her that night at the club, in the parking lot *after*... "You know her well?"

His laugh was sharp and full. "You jealous, darlin'?"

Dead pan, I smacked the candy from his hand. "Do I look it?"

"A little."

He wasn't wrong, which was the annoying part. As he stood from picking the package off the floor, he whispered in my ear. "I've never paid for it, baby. And she ain't got shit on you."

When I chose my candy, he took both to the counter and paid for them. Not revisiting the subject until we were halfway back to the bike and he was shaking candy from the pack into his mouth. It was like he had to think about it, decide if it was information he needed to give me. That he did that was damn frustrating.

"She's the one Archer messed around with." He spoke after he'd chewed and swallowed.

Of all the things I'd heard about my father, that was the least surprising. On the way home, I clung tight to Cam. As we roared past The Black Cat, I thought about that night. Not just the fight with Cam but also seeing the escort in the parking lot.

She hadn't touched Cam's vest or his hand. No, she'd touched the patch...the one that read Vice President. And the look on her face had been melancholy. How well had she known Archer?

A brightly lit storage facility, with a now familiar logo, screamed at me from the darkness. *Three-three-two*. Now I knew where the keycard came from. But what did I tell Cam? Now it was my turn to keep secrets, to decide what he needed to know. The Desert Kings were hanging from a thin rope...I didn't want to be the one to break it. Whatever was at the storage facility just might, though.

Eighteen

CAM

On the ride home, she seemed to stop second guessing this life and clung to me like wet leather. She fit perfectly, pressed against my back, as we screamed through the night.

The feeling of her there, safe and touching me, lifted the weight I'd shouldered for too damn long. She'd seen the real me and hadn't faltered. Damn if she hadn't got protective.

And said she wasn't leaving.

Fantasizing about a life with her was something I hadn't allowed myself to do. Now, it's all I could think about.

At home, she followed me up the stairs without question, her hand in mine. Like on the back of my bike, she fit there perfectly, too.

My anger from the frat house and from Preacher's shit had finally abated, chased away by this beautiful woman with hazel eyes that looked right through the worst parts of me and never blinked.

I shut the door behind her, locked it, and pulled her to me. Hugging her, I inhaled the apple-like scent she wore and ran my hands down her back. I'd been so scared I'd find her last night, like I'd found mom. I let myself process that fear and all I wanted was to touch her. Make sure she was real.

"I'm right here," she murmured and wrapped her arms all the way around me.

For almost a decade, I'd thought the MC had been everything I needed. I'd been wrong.

The thing I needed most was Riley Bowman.

Her lips were warm against my throat, across my jaw.

My apartment was suddenly too hot, and I pulled away from her long enough to shuck my cut, the hoodie, and the t-shirt.

Riley was already in my room before I could turn back to her. I followed, realizing I'd follow her anywhere she went, even if she left. I didn't think I'd be able to breathe without her. I'd go anywhere. Do anything.

If I was weak for it, so be it.

I caught her at the doorway, jerked her back, and scooped her into my arms.

"Cam!" But she was laughing as she rested her head against my chest.

On the bed, I laid her down and crawled on top of her, kissing her like I could memorize the taste of her, the feel of the slide of her tongue against mine. She tasted like candy, woman, and sex. All things that made my pulse roar in my ears and drown out all sound. God, how I wanted her.

The last time I'd been inside her had been frantic and dark. This time, I needed something else. I rolled off her and flicked on the bedside lamp.

"What are you doing?" She'd sat up and was kicking off her sneakers. Her cheeks were flushed by the wind and some of her hair had come out of the ponytail. She blew a piece out of her face and eyed me with uncertainty.

"I want to see what's mine."

In response, she pulled the hoodie and her shirt over her head, leaving just the bra and leggings.

I dipped a finger between her cleavage and hooked the front of her bra, tugging her to me. Without waiting for an invitation, she unclasped it.

My heart raced as I pulled it off. I could see her naked a thousand times, and each one would be like the first.

She was fucking amazing.

I sucked a nipple into my mouth and ran my hand down her side to her hip, then pulled her down with me. We rolled, so I was on top and I kissed my way down her stomach, dipped my tongue into her navel, then lower. I pulled the leggings and panties over her hips, all the way down her thighs.

"Cam." She wiggled under me, thrusting her hips upward. "Please."

That pretty pussy was so close, I couldn't resist.

I slid the tip of my tongue along her slit upward to flick her clit as I tossed the rest of her clothes to the floor. Naked beneath me, she moaned.

"This what you wanted, darlin'?" I made slow, easy circles while her scent left me rock fucking hard.

She bucked and made mewling sounds.

I chuckled and sucked her clit all the way into my mouth. Last night, she'd liked this part.

"Fuck, yes." She groaned.

With my hands under her ass, gripping both cheeks, I angled her up and feasted, suckling and licking while she gripped the blanket.

And when she bucked too fast, I pulled away and shucked my jeans and boxer briefs.

"What?" She screwed up her brow, confused and frustrated.

I almost laughed.

"I want to come inside you. So fucking bad."

The heavy lidded, sexy as fuck stare she leveled on me left my balls aching and my cock twitching.

"Do it."

Hearing her say it did me in every damn time.

"Roll over."

She did, glancing over her shoulder at me with those big, fuck me eyes. "On my knees?" Her long, slender body flared out at the hips, and my fingerprints were still red on her tight ass.

"Jesus." I swore. "Yes."

As she did, I clutched her hips and slid slowly inside her. I memorized the slick glide of her cunt over my cock, the wet warmth, the heady smell, the delicious fucking way she arched her back and moaned.

Fully sheathed inside her, I held us there, teasing us both, until it felt like my balls might explode. Then I took her with one full stroke out and back in, then another, fighting against the urge to fuck her until I couldn't see straight, and holding onto every little whimper and tremble.

Riley took me, learning quickly to rock backward to meet each thrust.

Goddamn, it felt good.

I wrapped her ponytail around my right hand and wrenched her head back, remembering the way her eyes had dilated at The Black

Cat when I'd grabbed her hair. Just a little pain...she liked that. Riley gasped, and trembling, arched her back in response.

The new angle let me slide in deeper, and her pussy clenched tight around me.

I almost came.

"Baby..." I whispered, relishing the heat of her wrapped around me, the way her ass bounced with each thrust, and moved faster.

She came a nanosecond before me, squeezing the come from my cock and bucking against me.

When we collapsed on the bed, I rolled to my side and pulled her snug against my chest.

"That was nice." She groaned after a few seconds.

"I've got a few more tricks up my sleeve." I kissed the slope between her neck and shoulder.

"I don't doubt that." She rolled in my arms, so that she was looking up at me.

Her expression was tender, her face sleepy. God, I could gaze down into those eyes for the rest of my life.

The thought ripped through me like barbed wire, tearing up everything as it went. What I'd thought of myself. Who I'd been. The life I thought I wanted.

Jesus. Fuck.

"What's wrong?" Never one to miss a thing, she leaned up on her elbow, frowning.

"Nothing." Of all the things I couldn't tell her, this was one I could. "You know how you think you know what you want from life, then someone shows up and tosses a big ass wrench into all of it?"

She snorted, grabbed the blanket, and pulled it over us, then lay back beside me. "Nothing in my life has gone according to plan. Absolutely nothing."

Then she examined me so long I adjusted my position beneath the blanket restlessly.

"Is this..." She gestured between us. "...the sex, all this is?"

There was no way she was serious. I waited a beat, but she said nothing else. I swore under my breath. "No. I can fuck anyone, Riley. You're..."

"The monkey wrench." She screwed up her nose like an annoyed rabbit.

"Yeah." I kissed the crinkly tip.

"Then I have to be more than something you own. I'm not property."

"You think so?" I brushed a stray lock of hair from her face.

"You've called me yours a few times. With Lance and now when we were..." Her face turned a pretty shade of pink. "I have to be equal in this relationship."

"Absofuckinglutely."

"*Cameron*, I'm serious."

"I kinda like it when you call me that."

Under the blanket, she punched me in the gut, but there wasn't a lot of force behind it.

"I'm naming my next wrench after you."

"Make sure it's pink handled."

I kissed her gently and reached over to cut off the light, shutting out the world and all the bullshit.

"Be serious."

I sobered. "Fine. Yes, there's more between us than just sex. No, I wouldn't have made the order to handle those assholes for just anyone." Any of the patch bunnies, nah, I wouldn't kill for them. But for Riley I'd rip a man limb from fucking limb.

A flurry of remembered anger thrashed about in my chest.

"I'm falling for you. I don't want to leave, I...want to be here, with you." She sounded half frightened, like she thought I'd balk and run.

"Darlin', I fell for you the first damn time I saw you." And it was the truth.

She wanted to be here with me. I hadn't scared her off. I damn sure didn't deserve her, yet here we were.

"I love you, Riley. I'm not on my way. I'm already there."

And it was fucking *terrifying*.

I kissed her mostly to keep her from saying something she might not be ready for. My tongue slowly exploring her mouth while her fingers traced circles on my chest. The hum of the AC pulled me from the kiss, and I tugged her closer so she wouldn't get cold.

"When I felt like I couldn't get to you in time, nothing else mattered. When I saw the marks he put on you—" I brushed my knuckles against the small bruises just above her collarbone. "—it took me to a dark place.

"You brought me back from there."

She nuzzled her face against my chest, speaking so quietly I almost couldn't hear her. "I feel like the truest version of myself when I'm with you."

"I don't need you to love me, Riley, but—"

"I do, I love you."

Whatever trepidation had been inside of me slid away.

"Then stay with me."

"I am."

Nineteen

Riley

"You sure about this?" Dylan stopped me on the sidewalk.

Downtown Dry Valley was busy, the weather nice, and people were outside on restaurant patios. In the distance, live music hummed.

It had taken several people to help me pull off a few hours to myself. Since the Desert Lights incident, Cam had stayed close. No backing out now.

"Absolutely."

"It's permanent." She prodded me again.

"I know." I stopped short of stomping my foot and rolling my eyes.

A smile blossomed on her pretty face. "Then, let's do this." She pulled open the door and the chimes tinkled.

Whatever I'd imagined a tattoo shop owned by an outlaw biker to look like inside, this wasn't it. The walls were painted a slate gray, framed original art dotted the walls with neon signs that were more coffee shop hipster than beer drinking biker. The floors were a dark stained wood, with a glossy finish, and the furniture in the waiting area was new and comfortable looking.

A large wooden counter with a glass front displaying piercing jewelry separated the front area from the four workstations behind it. A large, metal sign reading TATTOO hung on the wall behind a pretty bleach blonde covered in tattoos.

"Hey, Dylan, what can I do for you?"

"She's got an appointment with Puck."

"Cool, he's ready." She gestured past the empty chairs.

"They don't technically open until later," Dylan pointed out when she saw me checking out the place.

"Cam's girl gets special attention." Puck stood in a doorway at the back, a large mirror to his left.

My cheeks heated. "Thanks." into a private room, bigger than the others. The mirror wasn't a mirror at all, but rather two-way glass. One side of the room was a tidy office, the other side a clinical station.

He gestured for me to hop up on the tattoo chair. "Know what you want?"

"Sort of..." I explained while Dylan flipped through sketches on his desk.

"What if I do the letters like this..." He grabbed a pad, sketched out the word, then a snake sliding through a vine of pretty, rose-like flowers.

When I smiled, he continued until he'd shaded it in and was holding a beautiful piece of art in his large hands. The part that amazed me wasn't the speed at which he'd drawn it, but rather the intuitive way he seemed to know exactly what I wanted.

I leaned on my side in the chair, lifting my shirt so he could measure the length of my rib cage. Then he scanned the image, changed the shades on his laptop, the size, and printed it out on transfer paper.

He was pressing the printed image on my side when Dylan came back from a trip out for snacks.

On the other side of the glass, his employees came in, a motley crew of cool. A tall, slender, light-skinned Black man with a gorgeous sleeve of intricate designs. A white girl, with bright red hair and more color on her arms than any I'd ever seen, and piercings galore. And a white guy, in a polo shirt and khakis, with a preppy boy haircut, who looked ready to play golf, were it not for the huge gauges in his ears and the tattoos on his throat.

Clients came, too, making it easy to lose myself in the business of it as Puck slipped on latex gloves and set to work.

I didn't shout or make any sounds, but it stung until I got used to the discomfort. It felt more like a steady hum of dozens of bees stinging my side. Several hours later, I was standing in front of a full-length mirror on the back of his door admiring the handy work.

"This is...amazing."

The pride was obvious on his face. "It was my honor, Riley." Then he went through the aftercare process and covered it in clear plastic that stuck to my skin. "If you have any questions, give me a call. Savage knows what to do, though."

I turned and kissed him on the cheek, which left him blushing. "You're a badass, talented artist, Puck."

"He's not too shabby." Dylan tugged his beard before walking out.

"How much do I owe you?" I grabbed my purse and fished bills out of my wallet.

"Nothing." He waved me off, then gestured to his staff. "If you want to compensate, drop something in each of their tip jars. But I can't charge you."

"Well, thanks. This means a lot."

His amused smile followed me all the way out of the shop.

"I have something you need to wear tonight," Dylan said, driving me to her house rather than home.

The breezy shirt was white, with slits all the way up each side to my breasts, leaving my ribcage bare, and diving deep into my cleavage. Which I was glad to see I had again after several weeks of steady meals. I wore jeans and a pair of Dylan's brown, flat-bottomed cowboy boots.

I looked like a hot ass biker chick, tattoo and all. Like a kid with a new pair of shoes or checking out my hair after the first new color, I kept turning in the mirror to examine Puck's handiwork.

Cam's last name now ran the length of my side. A vine of rosettes and thorns intricately ran through each letter in one direction, a gold and black desert cobra in the other. To me, the perfect reflection of my time with him that showed exactly where I belonged.

"All good?" Dylan came into her bedroom.

After weeks of being surrounded by testosterone and Harleys, her little house was a breath of fresh, feminine air.

"Yeah, but if we don't get down to the clubhouse soon, Cam will probably come looking for me." He was getting restless. His tone when I'd spoken to him was resigned annoyance.

"I'm ready when you are." She snatched up her keys.

"What if he hates it?" Second thoughts rushed in as I followed her out.

"Then he's an asshole." In the Jeep, she continued. "But he's not, so he won't. To be honest, I think he's going to flip out in a good way."

As the sun set, she smiled. "With you, he's different. In a good way."

"Last time we went for a ride and talked about Cam, it didn't go so well," I reminded her.

Dylan laughed. "Then, let's not." She cranked up the radio as we drove.

My life could be like this all the time. I wasn't a bad person for wanting it, for refusing to let go of the happiness I'd found in Dry Valley with Cam.

The clubhouse was rocking, everyone milling about, readying to head to the fight—which wouldn't happen until later.

"Where will we be going?" I asked Dylan as we walked in.

"Out near Vegas, the Soletskys own a big warehouse out there that they've turned into a makeshift arena sort of deal."

Sounded like something the mafia would do. Because that's what they were, I'd realized. Just like in the old movies. The only thing they lacked was the Italian accent.

I looked for Cam immediately. He was by the pool tables, hip hitched on one of them, with a beer bottle hanging loosely in his right hand. Watching him from a distance, in his natural element, always gave me a little thrill. The patch bunnies hovered, but he paid them no attention. Instead, he chatted and laughed with Jester and his little brother.

Which, could be why the groupies were really hovering. The Vaughn brothers before a big fight were a hot commodity, apparently.

Cam turned in my direction, caught my gaze, and smiled. I beelined for him, kissing him as he wrapped a hand around my side. I dodged his fingers, moving them lower on my hip to keep him from touching the covering on my new ink.

He gave me a flirty look but continued his conversation.

Jester noticed the first. "Nice, sister." He tossed his chin over to Puck. "Well done!"

Cam, confused pulled away from me, taking my arm and spinning me like a dancer. I could tell the moment he saw the tattoo, because he stopped my spin and held me there, my arm in the air.

"Fuck"—He dropped my arm to pull the wispy white fabric away—"Me."

"You do this?" Still not addressing me, he shouted over the music to Puck, who grinned in response.

"Like I'd let anyone else." I jabbed his side with my fingers. "Like it?"

He pulled me against him, slid his hand down the center of my ass the way he'd done at Desert Lights, and massaged between my thighs. The press of his fingers on my most intimate spot, in front of all these people, sent a thrill up my spine.

"I fucking love it." And he kissed me, full of the heated promise of what would happen when we were alone.

Twenty

CAM

I had the pleasure of being seated at the table as the guys piled in...including Preacher. Riley couldn't have planned things better if she'd known where my head was. That she'd went so far as to tattoo my name on her skin, that her feelings ran that deep, made me a happy man.

That she'd decided to show me in a room full of Kings, especially Preacher? Well, that made a sort of pride curl and lick at my insides. It was the biggest middle finger I could have given the bastard.

I smiled at each of them as they walked in, even Preacher. My newfound attitude was confusing. This was the first time I'd sat at this table since Archer died and wasn't preparing for a fight.

At least, not here.

The burly old guy rolled with it, grinning as he took his seat. "Got a few things to say before Jester kicks some ass."

The table erupted into shouts and table thumping. Fight nights were where we cut loose, let the Ukrainians deal with the important shit.

"Bring cash boys! Bet big win big!" Jester shouted over the ruckus, then howled like a coyote.

"I got a couple on little brother to smoke your ass." Drop Top tossed bills onto the table, and the shit talking was on. Back and forth, they bet with each other, called each other names, but all in good fun. They needed this. *We* needed this.

Watching them reminded me why I'd joined the Desert Kings to begin with. Riley's surprise tattoo was like a glimpse of what life could be. *If* I could get shit sorted. These guys were my brothers, men I'd die for. Before Riley, the only family I knew.

I wouldn't let Preacher destroy them. Destroy *Us*.

"Alright. Settle down." Preacher rapped the gavel on the table a few times and the room quieted. "Listen, play nice tonight. No fighting outside the ring. I talked to the peckerwoods and Wanda wants to keep the peace, and make a good impression on the Ukrainians."

"Val and Ky don't give a shit about the peckerwoods." Merc's lip curled with obvious dislike. "They only invited them to put them in their place."

Preacher glowered at him. "It's in our best interest, monetarily, to make sure they get the chance. Wanda's promised that if we facilitate..."

"We voted on this before Archer died and shot it down. Then Ky did the same. We aren't hurting for cash, no reason to push for it," AP said simply, not intimidated at all.

"It's cool, Preach." I waved off Merc and AP's protest. "We can behave for one night. Doesn't hurt shit."

Across the table, Merc caught my gaze and gave a wolfish grin. We'd been friends for too long. He saw where this was going.

Time to stir the pot.

***

Riley rode behind me, sporting my leather, with my name permanently etched down her ribcage. She'd made a place for herself here with me. I'd love her forever for that alone. And despite all the Preacher shit; screaming down the highway with my brothers beside me and Riley behind me, I was fucking whole—happy.

The first time she'd ridden with me, I'd wished I could reach behind me and run my hand up her leg. I did now, down her shin and back up her calf. Then she covered my hand with hers. When I tugged her arm around me, she moved closer and ran her lips across the back of my neck.

It didn't matter that I rode with twenty other guys. We were the only two people who existed.

The warehouse was a huge, unmarked, metal monstrosity off the interstate. It dominated that part of the desert. The only other things around were a couple of truck stops. A cop sat near the entrance of one as we turned off.

He was paid well for his disinterest. Earning that money, he didn't even look up from his phone as we blew through the stop sign and into the parking lot. Other Kings were already there, along with a hell of a lot of people. The parking lot that wrapped around the building was packed.

"Strippers and whores must be good for business." Drop Top smirked after we parked on the sidewalk and shut off the motors.

"Nah, it's the drugs and guns," I whispered to Riley, half kidding.

From the open doors, the hum of excited conversation drifted out into the night.

"Check it out," I said to Riley as I climbed off my bike and held my hand for her to step off. She ditched the helmet, ran her hands through her hair, and looked around, eyes bright. I gestured to where Jester climbed off his bike and shouldered the backpack he'd had hooked to his seat. A line of scantily clad young women formed on the sidewalk, waiting to greet him.

His little brother walked out the open doors, grinning.

"Jester here is a local celebrity."

Riley snorted her disbelief and threaded her fingers through mine as I lit a cigarette with the other. "He's a regular Mike Tyson."

When Jester, blowing kisses to his fans, stepped through the door, the entire building erupted. The uproar shook the metal sides. I was rewarded with watching Riley's face change into one of absolute shock as she gaped. I brought our joined hands to her face and, asserting gentle pressure, pushed her chin up to close her mouth.

"Told you." I took another drag, waiting on the rest of the guys to roll off their bikes.

"This is insane."

"Yeah, he's been doing this awhile. Doesn't lose much. I think he was going to be a serious MMA fighter at one point but bailed." I finished my smoke and scuffed it out on the sidewalk before leading her into the fight.

The back side of the building was a row of closed doors bisected in the middle by a hallway—makeshift locker rooms and offices. Above them, several open-air viewing boxes that reminded me of the fairground horse races when I was a kid.

People filled every inch of available space. All different races and ethnicities. From peckerwoods to old school street thugs, college bitches to suits. I recognized a few cops, too.

And in the middle of it all was a giant octagon shaped cage with a mic hanging from the roof. That fighting ring was broadcast on giant flat screens at the top of each side of the building except above the viewing boxes.

I caught Ky Soletsky's gaze as he lounged against the cage, hands shoved in the pockets of his light-colored hoodie, grinning like the crazy European he was.

"Ky's fighting too, right?" Riley followed my gaze and half shouted her question.

The crowd had quieted, but not enough for me to hear her unless she spoke up.

"Yeah. Him, Jester, Crash, another Ukrainian guy, two guys from Vegas, and the two peckerwoods."

"Who are we putting money on?"

"That's a good question." Val Soletsky slapped a hand on my shoulder and one on Riley's.

For a split second, there was a glint of something terrible in his eyes. There wasn't a man alive that scared me, but Val came close.

Twenty-One

Riley

"First round, I'd bet high on the younger Vaughn," a familiar, accented voice said from behind me as a warm hand clasped my shoulder.

Cam cast a casual glance before cracking a grin, so I relaxed and went with it. I turned to Val Soletsky and smiled; it was hard not to. His eyes sparkled and his wolfish grin was bright, easy, almost boyish. The only thing about him that screamed monster was the designer sport coat and the large man beside him with more muscles than a Greek god.

"This is Bodhan. He and my nephew are my entries tonight. Bodhan will face young Bennett first."

The big man took Cam's hand in his beefy one and shook it, then nodded to me. But didn't seem to understand much outside of the introduction. He just looked around, unamused. The effect was eerie from such a spectacle of a man.

"He's huge." With tons of hulking muscle. "Bennett is..." I looked to where he stood on the outside of the ring, half hanging from the cage, joking with Ky. He was wearing a t-shirt with the sleeves and sides cut out of it, two sizes too big. He was muscular, sure, but lean like a teenager just after a growth spurt.

"Bodhan isn't as experienced a fighter, believe it or not. He didn't train until he came here, already grown. The Vaughns have done this their entire lives." He checked his phone and then grinned. "They'll be the first fight. Put your biggest bet on Vaughn." Val then motioned one of the bookies to us.

Cam put his arm over my shoulder. "I wouldn't argue with a Soletsky about a wager."

"Then I won't either." I put all the cash in my pocket on Bennett to win.

As I did, Val tapped two fingers on Cam's middle, drawing his gaze down, then pointed across the room. The motion was so quick that had I not been standing so close, even I wouldn't have seen it.

Cam's face changed, his jaw tensed, and the corner of his lip curled in a half snarl, half grin. It was so sexy I turned to follow his glare to a washed up, weathered looking woman with bleach blond hair and too much makeup. The only thing missing was the skinny cigarette dangling from her lips.

He dropped his arm from my shoulder and nudged me in the small of my back toward Val. "Stay with Val. I have to handle something."

The tone of his voice, barely audible over the crowd, made my stomach twist with anxiety. When I made to protest, he shook his head. "You'll have the best view in the house. This was the plan anyway, darlin'. I won't worry about you if I can see you up there."

"Please, Riley, be my guest." Val took me by the elbow and led me through the crowd, into that hallway, and up some stairs. With each step, people parted for us so that once he started moving, he didn't stop until we were seated in chairs overlooking the entire building.

Ky, the attractive younger Soletsky, gestured at the booth, then smacked a fist to his chest. Val mimicked the motion before sitting beside me.

"Do you fight as well?" Beneath the elder Soletsky's smooth exterior was something scrappy, like a fighter.

"He worries it'll mess up his pretty face." A man as big as Bodhan, with a baby face, sat on my other side. I'd seen him before, at the club.

"Yuri, meet Riley." Val gestured from me to the man. "He's my sparring partner. He tells himself that so that he doesn't feel so bad when I beat him."

But this big guy was more than that. When he shifted in his seat, I could make out the guns beneath his suit jacket. His gaze continuously flicked around the warehouse, no doubt focusing on the more dangerous players in attendance. Considering this was a den of vipers, he was a busy guy.

I shook the warm hand he offered. "Bodyguard."

"Smart girl," he said, his accent evident, and winked.

"Just how smart, I wonder?" Val questioned, nodding toward the crowd. "Tell me, what do you see?"

I searched the crowd, looking for Cam in part, wondering what Val wanted me to see. Jester leaned over the ropes, shouting into Bennett's ears. His brother, looking bored, shoved in his mouth guard and rolled his shoulders. Across the ring, the Ukrainians made a big deal of Bodhan in his corner. But beneath him, peckerwoods milled about. Two of them had been at the bar with Cam and I not long ago, he'd nearly shot one.

But there was something about the way they hovered that reminded me of vultures circling their next meal.

"They're hoping Bodhan destroys Bennett."

Val nodded, pleased. "But he won't. What I wonder is *why*."

Jester had walked in here, king of the castle. This was his domain, where he shined. Bennett was an extension of that. "To weaken Jester?"

This time, Val beamed at me. "Good. Smart. What else?"

I blinked at him, as if I didn't quite understand. But maybe I did. Cam was easy to see, directly across from me, arms folded across his chest, and gaze hard. He watched the vultures. So did Merc beside him. Even Jester cast glances in their direction. In truth, all the Desert Kings were tense around the peckerwoods.

All but one. Preacher stood not far from one of their fighters, talking with a group of people I'd never seen before. He didn't stay long, peeling away and off to someone else. Almost as if he didn't want to be seen talking to anyone.

I didn't like it. But I wasn't about to say something like that to Val. I'd learned that lesson.

"What makes Jester so special?" I asked instead, keeping my thoughts to myself as both fighters in the ring stood up and readied themselves.

"He's that good." Val leaned forward in his seat, eagerly anticipating Bennett and Bodhan's fight.

Nervous for the kid, not the loss of money, I hugged my middle.

I shouldn't have worried at all. Bennett moved fast, throwing punches to Bodhan's middle quicker than the other man could take a step. Then to his face, his head, until Bodhan swayed around confused and dizzy.

The bulky man threw a few punches, clocking the kid in the face once. Bennett's gleeful laugh echoed over the crowd. He fought with more than his fists then, kicking the big man until he dropped to his knees and fell over.

Bennet pounced then, flipping the guy to his side and wrapping him up with his legs, pulling his opponent's arm to an impossible angle. Bodhan's face turned red, screwed up with pain, as Bennett shouted wordlessly and pulled more.

When Bodhan patted Bennett's arm with a quick smack, the ref separated them, and lifted Bennett's arm as the Ukrainians collected Bodhan from the ring.

Less than three rounds and the kid won.

"Wow."

Val gestured to a man who appeared behind us. "Collect for Riley as well."

"You voted against yourself?" I was surprised.

"Of course. I like money." Val laughed happily.

Cash found its way to my hands, more than I'd started out with, more than I'd held in my entire life. For that, I listened to Val for the next few fights. I bet on Jester, on Ky, and on a smarmy looking peckerwood even though it made me vomit in my mouth a little.

Bennett and Ky fought in the next round. Val hadn't been much help there, and I'd lost money betting on Jester's baby brother. He was good, but Soletsky was bigger *and* better. Val had swelled with pride then, even standing and leaning over the railing to shout and cheer in his native tongue. The burst of emotion was a pleasant surprise and fun to watch.

When Jester eviscerated Wanda's fighter, leaving the peckerwood in a puddle of blood in the middle of the mat, there was chaos. A bottle flew by Jester's head, crashing into the crowd. Leather vests clashed with sleeveless t-shirts as Wanda's boys went after the Desert Kings.

It happened so fast, but I'd been watching closely. The pecker-woods hadn't made the first move—Merc had thrown the first punch. A haymaker, to the face of a guy on the corner of the ring, seconds before the bottle had flown.

Beside me, Yuri barked orders in his native language. Val kept his intense gaze on the fighting beneath us. Seemingly unconcerned, but he'd stopped talking.

I lost Cam in the ebb and flow of the fight.

But found Preacher, easily, he and his flunky stood on the fringe, not far from Wanda. Ghost pushed people away, but didn't fight like the rest of the guys. I didn't like it. Val followed my gaze, and as if he could feel us watching him, Preacher shouldered into the crowd.

"I liked your father. This one," Val cast a glare toward Preacher, pulling Puck off a peckerwood beneath us, then across the room. "Not so much."

The brawl continued, the ref standing in the middle of the ring, watching wide-eyed. The Ukrainians did little to stop it.

A familiar figure with black hair entered through the main door and surveyed the havoc unbothered. He was surrounded by a crew of unassuming men in non-descript but expensive clothes. I'd met him before.

Santos Garza.

Frantically, I stood and searched for Cam. I didn't know this man, but I got the distinct feeling he shouldn't be here. Or that him being here was some sort of bad omen. One of Val's men leaned over his shoulder and whispered in his ear, drawing his attention to Garza.

Beneath us, Garza tossed a toothy smile to Val, who barely grinned. As if he didn't want me to know he was pleased.

Finally, Val gave a curt nod, and men in dark suits moved through the fighting. Some escorting bystanders out, others seeming to cull small sections of men throwing punches. Because it was exactly that. Thirty or more guys, over half wearing dark vests like Cam, fighting. Nothing like those in the ring.

Except for Jester, shirtless atop a guy in red flannel with no sleeves, beating him bloody. The blood splattering brought back a memory that left me cold. I leaned against the railing and squeezed my eyes shut, my heart beating in a panicked rhythm in my chest.

When I opened then I saw Cam, stalking toward me through the fighting. He dodged punches, threw some, and when the crowd surged against him, he battled through it like some sort of dark knight. *Mine.*

Knowing he'd be with me in only a short jog up the steps, I glanced for the others in time to see Preacher slip out the side doors with a goon or two, and Wanda herself.

The hair on the back of my neck prickled.

Cam reached the steps beneath me about the same time as Garza. They spoke briefly before Cam charged up to me. He was breathing heavy, his hair messy, and there was blood on his bottom lip and a little on his knuckles.

He looked every bit the wild boy I was madly in love with.

"Thanks, Soletsky." He nodded toward me.

"I appreciate the heads up," Val leaned back, smug.

I glanced between them as understanding dawned. Cam had known this would happen, and so had Val. But why?

"Think you kicked up enough ants?" Val asked as he stood. Behind Cam, Yuri gave Garza and the two men with him a quick pat down.

Cam's reaction was to grin wide and take my hand.

As we passed Garza, he gestured for Cam to wait.

"I'm wondering, Savage, if you know where your president ran off to? I was hoping for a word with him."

Cam shrugged a shoulder. "Not a clue, haven't seen him in a while."

It was obvious by the narrow gaze and frown, Garza wasn't happy with that response.

I waited until we were outside to jerk Cam to a stop. "Preacher left with that Wanda lady and a few other MC guys before the fight was over." I spit it all out on a fast exhale as people spilled out behind us. One of which was Merc, who heard every word I said.

Realizing my mistake, I flinched. But this time Cam didn't mind. He looked past me to Merc. "You think anyone else saw that?"

"Doubt it." The roar of Harleys echoed in the distance. "But he sure made a quick getaway when the Cartel showed." Cam climbed on his bike and pulled me on the back. "Let's see if he beats us back to the clubhouse."

Twenty-Two

CAM

The freedom and reverberation of the ride had always chased away everything. If something bothered me, a long ride could fix it. Here lately, the only thing that did that was Riley.

Now, the angry growl matched my mood as I shifted gears and accelerated into the night.

I squeezed Riley's knee as I changed lanes, casting a quick glance in the mirror at the bikes that followed us. Riding in a large group like this drew attention, but in Hayes County we were invincible.

Except from the inside. Preacher was a cancer. If I'd needed proof, I had it now.

There was a time he'd have jumped in that fight, just like the rest of us. Now he'd have some explaining to do—I had my proof he was putting his own shit above the Kings. That wouldn't fly.

A different kind of fight was coming, and I was more than ready for it.

Preacher's bike wasn't in the parking lot as I whipped in. No one's was. Behind me, the lot filled up fast. The whoops and shouts echoed across the desert as bike engines shut down and guys climbed off. This level of testosterone and adrenaline were cause for celebration.

I pulled Riley to my side and lit a cigarette as I turned back to watch the revelry. I never thought I could lose all of this, all of them. But I would if it meant this...that the Kings remained. The finality of that decision broke something inside me.

"They're happy." She chuckled, surprise lifting her brow.

"A good fight always boosts morale." The sound of her voice was a soothing balm. It was unfair of me to count on that to keep me whole if I lost this.

Inside, Dylan was sitting on the bar with a beer bottle in hand, and her feet swinging. The eerie quiet fit her, like a calm before the storm. *Family.* "I heard y'all made a mess of Wanda's boys."

"You damn right we did!" someone shouted from the door as others spilled in.

The Desert Kings had wanted this fight since the day they'd chased Riley and me. Preacher denying that taste for blood would be his downfall. Merc's plan had been executed to perfection.

Almost immediately, the clubhouse was rocking with music and people—patches and groupies alike. Friends of the club who'd been at the fight were here, too. I sat at a round booth in the corner facing the door, the one Preacher himself often sat at, my arm over Riley's shoulder. It was a statement; one Merc didn't miss.

He slid into the booth and whistled. "Jester texted me, stopped by his house to drop his shit off and Preacher rode by—heading out from the Bends."

The twisty, turning road lined with trailer parks that hugged the dried-up riverbed. Peckerwood central. I appreciated the heads up but didn't need it. I was tense enough.

Riley didn't ask me what was up, but her fingers trembled when she dropped a hand to my knee beneath the table. I picked those elegant digits up and brought them to my lips.

"I won't let anything happen to you."

"It's not me I'm worried about." She cast a nervous glance up at me. The confrontation was coming. She knew it and didn't like it.

I kissed her fingers again, placed her hand back in my lap, then nuzzled her head. "I have to do this, baby."

"I know."

Even if she didn't, she understood. It was that part of Riley that had made me care so much so fast. Fuck if she didn't understand me all the damn time.

It was several minutes before the door was flung open. Drop Top blustered and stalked across the room, slapped a hand on the bar, and barked orders at Dylan. When he looked at me, it was with a half accusatory, half curious glance. His already disorderly frizzy hair had sprouted from the tie in the back, and he was sporting a mostly black eye.

The grimy bastard hated fights. Mostly because he always got his ass kicked. Those short little arms didn't swing very far.

Regardless of what he thought, even the old fucker had fought with us.

Dylan cut the music with a remote, just as AP joined Drop Top at the bar. His annoyance was evident in the bristle of his back. He didn't like the way the other man was talking to his daughter. I couldn't hear their quiet argument over the din of nervous conversation as people looked around.

"Chapel, now!" Preacher boomed as he pushed open the door and let it slam shut behind, like he was some sort of fucked up biker messiah.

Drop Top turned toward the back hallway, Preacher's bitch Paul followed. But nobody else moved. Dekes leaned against the pool table and propped the cue under his chin. "Brother, it's a party, relax."

The vein in Preacher's neck popped. He was the hothead, always had been. As a probie, I'd learned to read him. It was a damn good thing, too. I was out of the booth before Preacher could take a step, and in front of Dekes before he could jerk him up. His fat fingers clenched into a fist in front of my face.

I grinned in challenge. *Do it.* One swing was all I needed, and I'd lay his old ass out, right here in front of everyone. Vice President be damned.

"He's right, Preach." Jester came up behind him. "I won, and we fucked some peckerwoods up. It was a good night."

"Chapel," he growled.

When he tried to shoulder past me, I was ready for it. I didn't move, his beefy body half bouncing off me. He sputtered and stomped into the room, followed by his two flunkies.

The rest of the table glanced at me, waiting for me to decide what came next. Even AP. On a sigh with a half grin, I lit a cigarette and shrugged.

I made him wait, watching the minute hand tick by on the giant neon clock over the door. At three, I turned toward Riley, pulled her close, and kissed her. The tender press of her lips was the sort of thing I'd never expected from this life. . "Have Dylan take you home."

"I'm not going anywhere." She tilted her chin in a proud way that reminded me of Archer. I could demand she go back, turn the simmering anger inside me on her. And no doubt she'd do as I said. But what would it cost her?

I leaned down to her ear. "Listen, I need to go in here and take care of shit without worrying about you being here if it goes sideways. Please go home."

She pressed her lips to mine. "Don't make me wait long."

"I won't." I watched her walk to Dylan, whose brow was creased with worry.

Then I motioned the other guys toward the Tribute Hall. I was the last one to enter the room, making damn sure Dylan and Riley were leaving. Everyone else was at their seat. I kicked the door shut with the back of my heel and went to mine, spinning it around backward, and straddled it.

It was an insolent move, knowing Preacher hated the sound of the chair dragging across the floor as much as he'd hated having to wait on me. I crushed my cigarette out in the ashtray on the table and blew my smoke right at him. I fucking smiled as I did it.

"I don't know which one of you started that stupid shit at the fight—"

"Peckerwoods started it when they came after Cam," Puck stated simply.

Preacher glowered at him. "And we settled that. Starting a full out brawl at an event is bullshit. I'm trying to keep peace in the Valley, not start a god damned war."

"That why you dipped out the back with Wanda?" I didn't wait for him to get a full head of steam.

"Who said I did? Your little princess up there with Soletsky? After you told us she wasn't going to be a problem? Now the little bitch is lying on me?"

I jumped across the table, slapping the gavel so that it flew against the wall, and shoved him in the chest so hard the chair clattered from beneath him, and he spilled onto the floor. Someone jerked me back across the table, and Puck grabbed my fist before I could shove it into the bastard's red, sputtering face.

He jumped to his feet as several guys pulled me away. I shook with anger, hatred, and the overwhelming desire to beat the fucking shit out of him.

"She wasn't the only one who saw you," AP drawled lazily. "And fuck face here was with you." He tossed a hand toward Paul.

The younger man's face went tight, and he said absolutely nothing.

I shrugged out of Puck's grasp. "Call her a liar again. I fucking dare you."

"Sit down, boy," Preacher snarled, standing behind his chair now. He definitely wasn't moving closer to me. "You've caused enough problems. Your shit after the cartel meet and starting this shit tonight is going to tear this club apart."

"The only person doing that is you," I said with a sneer.

"Me?" His eyes flew wide, actual shock registering on his face. "I'm not the one palling around with the fucking cartel and bringing that shit into the Valley."

"Nah, *brother*, Garza showed up looking for you. Personal business. Care to share that with the rest of the table?"

It seemed all the air sucked out of the room, and he narrowed his eyes on me. "You got something else bothering you, *son*?"

Yeah, you killed Archer, you piece of shit. I just couldn't prove it yet.

"I want to know why you're so chummy with the fuckers who try to undercut our business and pose the biggest threat to the club—hell, to the whole damn county." I was shouting now and didn't fucking care.

"From where I'm standing, boy, the biggest threat is in this room." He had no idea. But it wasn't me.

"I move for a cool down, meet back here in forty-eight hours, and hash it all back out." This from Drop Top, who now looked impossibly old and desperately tired.

"I second it." AP stood. "And everything stays in this room. I shouldn't have to remind any of you reprobates."

Preacher stormed out, Paul on his heels.

Drop Top laid his head on the table. "I don't have time for this shit, man," he whined, but he got up with the rest of the table and walked out.

Before I could leave, Merc stood and shook his head. I lingered and lit a cigarette.

At a wordless gesture from his father, Merc shut the door behind Jester.

"What the fuck is wrong with you?" AP's usually calm demeanor cracked. Shock and anger echoed in his voice.

I lowered myself slowly into my seat, head down, taking a calming drag as I did. If AP Merrick was shouting at me, I'd fucked up.

Only four of us remained at the table. Dekes lounged back in his seat, lighting a small cigar. One whiff of the aromatic smoke told me it wasn't tobacco. I took a long hit when he passed it to me and thought about my next move.

"He shouldn't be president." I passed it to Merc.

I was still pissed about Preacher's shit talking Riley—again. About all of it, if I was being honest, my anger was turning quickly into hatred.

"You still can't go around throwing punches in chapel, kid." AP's voice was quieter now, like he was too tired to be having this conversation. "Not after he's already tried to come for your patch."

"Not like Preach was going to throw any tonight for the Kings." Dekes took the blunt from Merc when AP refrained.

"He's doing a lot of sketchy shit, Dad. Likely he's the reason the peckerwoods went after Cam and Riley."

AP sighed. "That doesn't excuse what Cam did. He'll have to pay for that."

"We caught him in a lie," I pointed out. "When does he pay?"

"And nobody's going to remember that because you blew your top." AP settled a hard, fatherly gaze on me.

"I'll remember it, so will Puck and Jester." Dekes surprised me with the unwavering support. "When we sit down, I'll use it to call for a new vote. Never liked that bastard being near the head of the table, anyway."

"And who are you nominating in his place?" AP asked, tossing his hands up.

"The kid." Dekes shook an elbow toward me.

"No." I took a hit, then passed it. I was mentally halfway out the fucking door without Archer here. "I don't want it, but I'm not going to sit quietly with Preacher at the helm."

AP rolled his eyes. "Son, you can't just blow-up what Archer built because you're shacked up with his daughter and Preacher doesn't like it. This club, what it means to all of us, to this town—it's too important for a childish pissing contest."

I spun the keys to Archer's bike between my fingers, missing him more than I thought I could miss anyone. "It's more than that." I held his gaze. "Archer didn't shoot himself, and I'm pretty sure I know who did."

Dekes choked and coughed, shocked. Which I'd expected. What I didn't expect was AP's lack of reaction.

He wasn't surprised at all. "You've got two days to ."

"Then we handle it." Dekes crushed out the roach.

Merc stopped me at the door. "What if we can't prove it?"

I shrugged. "Then I'm out."

Twenty-Three

Riley

Something big and dangerous was churning like a storm on the horizon. I could sense it the moment I told Cam that Preacher had slipped out the door with Wanda rather than join the rest of them in the brawl.

But he'd come home to me, in one piece, after the meeting. We'd made love. Unlike most nights, he hadn't slept after. He'd tossed and turned, restless beside me, until the sun came up. So, I didn't wake him and laid beside him, comforted by the quiet hum of the air conditioner, until midmorning.

Cam was beautiful, laying there with the sheets wrapped around his waist, strips of sunlight snaking through the blinds in strips across his back. His eyes were closed, but he wasn't asleep. He'd stretched, licked his lips, and lay there quietly.

I traced the lines of the skull tattoo on his shoulder, across the gilded lines of the broken crown.

"What would you think if I went Nomad, and we left to start a life somewhere else?"

"Nomad?" I dragged my fingers lower, tracing the dip his spine took at his lower back. Touching him openly, whenever and wherever I wanted, was a thrilling delight I didn't think I'd ever get used to. Knowing that he wanted a life with me was something else entirely.

"I'd keep the cut, the patch, but wouldn't belong to a charter." He rolled to his side to face me and wrapped an arm over my hip beneath the sheet.

"Will they just let you?" I didn't know all his secrets, but he definitely knew all of theirs. I snuggled against his chest, content in the warmth of him.

His voice turned dark, haunted. "I'll take care of it."

Could he really leave? That was the scariest part. That they wouldn't let him. Even if he could, how did I tell him I wanted to stay? I felt at home here. This was the life I wanted. And even if I found the words, there were too many secrets piling up between us. There were things he couldn't tell me and things I was afraid to tell him.

In this, I understood the fear of the Desert Kings, of what they could do. I'd seen it firsthand. I couldn't act on assumptions and half-baked theories.

"What if I want to stay?"

"In Dry Valley?" Surprise lifted his voice.

"Here, with you, is the first time in my life I've felt like I belonged."

He nuzzled the top of my head in the way that left me feeling safe, secure, and warm low in my belly.

"Besides, Boyd Law School is in Vegas."

He chuckled at that, nudged his leg between my knees against the core of me, and kissed me. His warm lips were soft at first but grew increasingly more demanding, and I found myself grinding my hips against his thigh, wishing I weren't wearing panties.

Cam had a way of making me forget we were having a serious conversation.

He shifted, rolled me onto my side, and kissed down my neck. "That smart shit is sexy. You going to let me do bad things to you while you write dissertations?" He nipped at my nipple through the thin t-shirt I'd worn to bed.

Laughter bubbled up with my moan. "Be serious for a second. If I wanted to stay here...how do we make it happen?"

"I need proof Archer didn't kill himself." It was what he didn't say that hung so heavy.

"Proof?"

Cam squeezed his eyes shut. "Yeah."

I thought about all the little things that were bothering me. And only one was tangible. "I don't have that, but I may have a lead." I might have shoved the box of books into a corner, but the keycard had stayed at the forefront of my mind.

I scrambled from Cam's bed, jogged down the stairs to the main house, and back so fast I was breathless and my cheeks red when I returned. He'd sat up and opened the blinds so that sunlight lit up the room. His hair was a little messy but did nothing to deter from his sex appeal. Crawling onto the bed, I settled beside him.

"I found this in some of Archer's things." I told him about the significance of the book and where I'd seen it at the lawyer's office. "I saw this place last night, right near the motel where he died."

"I know what we're doing today." Cam shook his head in disbelief.

Cam's wicked grin turned my insides to lava as he tossed the keycard onto the bedside table.

"And I know how we're getting started." He pushed me onto my back and climbed on top of me, kissing all the way down my shirt and jerking my panties off. He nipped at my inner thighs as I gasped.

"I think I really like how this day is starting off." I squeaked, and my cheeks heated as he glanced up from between my thighs.

Then he kissed my slit, licking and sucking my lips between his while my hips bucked. With no warning, his tongue whipped up and circled the apex of my pleasure. He drove me mad with his mouth, over and over until I was shouting and bucking, coming hard against his face.

He chuckled and climbed up my body, raking his cock across my inner thigh. I wanted it so bad. No condoms anymore, never again, just the friction of his slick skin against mine. When I bucked up to meet him, he nipped at my bottom lip. Then kissed me, hard, sucking my tongue into his mouth as he slid his cock inside me. I groaned and gripped his thighs. He tore his mouth from mine on a pant and a moan.

"I don't know which I love more, the way you taste or the way you feel around my cock."

I could only gasp, because I didn't know the answer to that one either. Didn't care, so long as he didn't stop. He moved slowly, pulling all the way out of me, then diving back in.

"Fuck." It was my turn to groan.

He braced his arms on either side of my head, pumping slowly still, teasing me. When I mewled a complaint, he dragged my bottom lip down with his thumb. "Tell me what you want, baby."

"More, faster." I gasped.

He obliged, but not before changing our position, tossing my legs over one shoulder and turning my hips a little. Suddenly he was bigger, harder, and I felt so impossibly tight that I feared I'd squeeze him out of me.

When I protested, he shushed me with that same thumb, drove himself all the way into me, then held still. He traced the light bruises just over my collar bone and his eyes darkened.

"Nobody ever touches you again." His voice was different, strained in a way that made him sound like a desperate animal.

I took his hand, placed it at the front of my throat, and rolled my hips. I never wanted to think of Lance again. Only Cam. Always Cam. Like that night never happened.

He watched me for a moment, then closed his eyes. Slowly, like he understood, he wrapped his long fingers around my throat, and undulated his hips in a way that sent pleasure spiraling outward from my core.

When I pressed against his hand, he gripped a little tighter. I could breathe, I could *feel*.

Then he pinned my head to the pillow. White hot sensation lit up my spine. The feel of him moving inside me, the stark power imbalance of the way he held me, all of it washed away any memory I had of that frat party.

Nothing else existed but Cam.

"Tighter." I gasped, wrapping one hand around his wrist. He'd asked me once if I'd want to be choked. I'd thought no. But now, with Cam... "Please. Faster."

His eyes flicked open, pleasure and desire flaring inside them. He did as I asked, stealing my breath with a strong squeeze of his long fingers. I pressed against that touch, embraced the fear and pleasure all rolled into one.

Cam thrust faster, panting, his eyes narrowing the way they did right before he came. With each thrust I was closer, growing light-headed, shaking.

And as he exploded inside me, filling me with liquid heat, I came on a wordless cry, Cam's touch stealing everything.

He let go, dropping my legs and falling behind me, curling around me.

"Fuck me, you're amazing." He kissed the back of my neck, stroked down my hip with his hand.

"Not too bad yourself." I chuckled, pulling his arms around me. "You can do all of that, anytime."

"Getting a little kinky there, darlin'." He nibbled across my shoulder. "Makes me think I need to show you a few more things."

I snorted a laugh, but really, I *was* curious.

"Maybe you should."

Twenty-Four

Riley

I didn't let my gaze linger on the motel when we pulled up to the storage place. Cam drew my attention. There was a level of hope in him that had been missing the past few days. He was back to being my beautiful boy, kicking out the kickstand and holding my hand as I climbed from behind him. No furrowed brow, no lines on his forehead. We both believed there were answers here.

Had to be, because we didn't have anything else.

The lobby of the office was cool and smelled of Pine-Sol and cardboard from the wall of flat boxes for purchase. It reminded me of the first day of school and put me instantly at ease.

I smiled at the bored looking young woman at the counter as we approached. She seemed to ignore me completely, letting her gaze linger on Cam. I had already noticed that the leather vest made most people in Dry Valley take notice. But we were just outside of town now, closer to the city, and she wasn't the least bit put off. Quite the opposite.

Ignoring her ogling, I laid the keycard on the counter. "Hi, good afternoon. Could you tell me if this keycard is for a unit here?" Cam had said the place was a chain all over Nevada.

She glanced down at the card, typed the numbers on it into her computer on the counter, then narrowed her eyes at me. "Do you have photo identification?"

"I do." I slid her my ID.

She didn't bother looking at it, just shrugged. "It's company policy to not give out customer information except to the renter themselves."

"Good thing I don't need any of his information." I took a deep breath. "My father, Rick Bowman, rented this unit. He passed away last month. I'm tying up all the loose ends and need to know if it's here. I can walk up and down every aisle if you want me to, but I was hoping you could make this easier."

"Do you have the ?"

No, and we didn't have another week or more to wait on it to come in the mail.

"Not yet."

"Come back when you do. I can't help you until then."

I stood gaping at her as she turned back to the tablet she'd been reading on. The skin on my chest and around my neck grew hot. Not because she was following the rules, but because she'd written my request off and acted is if I was no longer there.

Cam, phone in hand, leaned over the counter.

"Hey there, sweetheart." He made a show of looking for a name tag. "Your name is...?"

"Kelsy." She smiled at him, blushing a little.

"That's a very pretty name."

She practically preened, and I rolled my eyes.

I'd seen him do this before and didn't need to watch him do it now. Mostly because I wanted it to work and didn't want my annoyance to show. So, I walked out front and glanced back at the two-story climate-controlled facility and the rows of red-doored storage units behind it.

I wasn't jealous. Cam had zero interest in the girl. She was years younger than me, even. But that she was so quick to be lulled into whatever flirtations some hot guy tossed her way pissed me off. She should be smarter than that.

Had I been?

A few seconds later, the door dinged as Cam walked out and waved the key card at me. "Upstairs, second floor of the climate-controlled units. Keycard will open the main door, too."

"Are you serious? She gave it up that easy?"

He chuckled. "Yup. Like magic." He waved his fingers around in front of me and danced a few steps away to avoid my halfhearted punch at his middle.

"Don't gloat, it makes you less sexy."

He snorted, tapped the card on the pad, and pulled the door wide to hold it for me. Inside and up the stairs, everything smelled of sterile cleaner and packaging materials—just like the front office. Above us, the lights were bright and the only sound was the humming of the air conditioners.

I counted as we walked, stopping at unit three-three-two, and waited as he tried the card.

I don't know what I'd expected, but a mostly empty unit hadn't been it. For a minute, I thought there was nothing there, until Cam flicked on the light, and I saw the large safe with a digital number pad in the back.

"Whoa."

"Gun safe." Cam's steps echoed on the polished concrete as he walked up to it. "What do you think the combination would be?"

"No idea. I didn't see anything in the book when I found the key, either. But you should try some numbers that might mean something to him. You knew him, I didn't."

Cam knelt in front of the safe and tried a few combinations. Each one was followed by a rapid succession of beeps that told us those numbers were wrong. "What's your birthdate?"

I told him. He keyed it in but got the same beeping. Then he keyed in something else, and the door popped open. He held it, hesitating.

"My birthday?"

"And mine, together."

His quiet words were a gut punch. Archer had loved us both. I was learning, slowly, that Cam might have been right. Archer's love for me was why he'd stayed away, to protect me.

I was beginning to understand from what.

"Pull the door down."

I did, with a rattling clang as he flicked on his phone's flashlight.

"You ready?"

"Yes." Why was I shaking?

The door swung open with a little whoosh. Inside, it was packed with stacks of cash. Each shelf lined with neatly bundled bills. Cam took one and handed it to me. "Each stack is ten thousand."

Then he whistled. "There was always this rumor, especially when I was young, that Archer and Preacher had done some twisted shit out in the desert before they started the club. Made bank doing it. I always thought it was bullshit, because why live like this when they had that kind of cash?"

"Because control of the town was more important."

"I guess so." He pulled out a few stacks, shoved them in his vest pocket, and shut the door.

I took a deep breath of stale, storage unit air. But it didn't make me feel any better. "Now we know what Preacher has been looking for."

We locked everything back up, and Cam handed me the keycard as we walked back out to the bike. Cam had been silent the whole time. I was...shocked and a little scared. I wasn't sure how deep that gun safe was, but there was easily more than a million dollars in there.

"Keep that card on you. Always." Cam stopped at the bike and stared across the street at the motel.

Early in the evening, it was already busy. Too expensive for the addicts, a mix of weary travelers from the interstate and what I could only imagine were well dressed prostitutes moved in and out.

A dark SUV I recognized pulled into the parking lot, one I'd seen that night at The Black Cat. A woman, even more familiar, stepped from inside. The escort was showing up more and more.

When Cam fired up the bike, she jumped, startled, and looked back at us, her hand up in a half wave.

She'd known Archer. Maybe she'd been with him the night he died.

***

Cam was quiet when we got back. I didn't push. He'd talk when he was ready—when he'd processed everything. All the dots were connecting and a clear image was forming for both of us.

Preacher had killed my father for the money. Now, he was set on intimidating me into telling him where it was.

"Is this the proof you need?"

Leaning against the sink in a kitchen that was beginning to feel like my own, he stared out the window into the backyard. Much like he'd watched the motel before we drove home.

"No."

"But it's obvious he's been after the money the whole time, trying to scare me into telling him about it—or giving it to him, even. The break in, his weird interrogation, always wanting me alone."

"Doesn't matter. We can't tell anyone about the money."

"Why not? I thought part of being a Desert King meant keeping nothing from them."

"*Riley.* Think about it. That type of money makes a lot of enemies. Archer was killed for it."

He was right and believed that with my entire soul. "So, what now?"

"I don't know. Leave? Start a new life, nothing stopping us now. We can go wherever, be whoever we want to be."

I stood beside him and rested the side of my head against his shoulder. "I'll go wherever you go." We'd talked earlier about what this place had come to mean to me.

"Change your mind about staying here?"

"No." I snuggled in when he wrapped his arm around me. "It's not this house, or Dry Valley. My home...is you." Because life without him scared me more than I'd like to admit. My future wasn't uncertain as it had been when Mom was sick. It was a deeper fear than that. I don't know if I could live without Cam.

"When my mom was dying, it was one bad thing after another. I finally just wanted it to be over, even if it meant she was gone and I was alone. I didn't want her in pain. I didn't want either of us to suffer. I just wanted it to stop. Then it did, and I was alone, with nothing. And it was scarier than the unknown had been."

He turned so that he could hug me against his chest. Pressing my face there, I grounded myself in the scent of him, in the feel of his steady heartbeat against my cheek, and the strength of the arms that held me tight.

Cam didn't say anything, just let me talk. I don't know who needed that more, me or him.

"Then I met you. Everything changed. I can imagine a future now, a life. But it has to be with you..." I lost the rest of my words in a tremble of emotion.

"Anywhere you go, I go," he finished for me.

I nodded against him.

When I felt steady again, I pulled away. "Why was Archer at that motel? Did it have anything to do with the money?" Pretty sure I already had my answer.

"I doubt it." He flinched a little, poured a glass of water from the tap, drank half of it, and contemplated the remnants. All as if he wanted to avoid this conversation. That he was uncomfortable amused me.

"Was he meeting the hooker we saw at the gas station?" I tried not to smile.

Cam set the glass down and cast a sideways glance at me. "Probably."

"So that's why Merc said the Soletsky's were worried about their girls."

Cam's face rolled through several expressions: annoyance, shock, amusement, and finally pride. It was the last one that made my heart jump a happy beat.

"That night when I was with Merc on the porch, you were listening."

I ducked my head, feigned contrition. "I was scared and curious."

"Worried I'd tell him I just banged the hot virgin?"

"No—yes, maybe."

With a laugh, he tugged me close and kissed me. "I'd never have done that. All you are, all of this? It's just mine."

"There you go, getting all possessive again."

"You're the one with my name etched into your skin" He gently stroked his knuckles down my tender side.

"There's some shit I need to do before tomorrow," he whispered against my hair after we'd stood there, holding each other for a while.

"Okay."

Twenty-Five

CAM

There was only one person I trusted to watch my back in The Bends and that was Merc. In the same breath, I'd left Riley with his sister. Preacher wouldn't fuck with AP's kid. Not after the last chapel.

The twisting, one lane road was filled with more potholes than the entirety of Hayes County. Every bump shouted how little people thought of this place. Which was a mistake that Wanda Haynes had taken advantage of.

They didn't call the cops in the Bends. Whatever shit was flushed here stayed and festered.

"You sure about this?" Merc asked as I steered the blacked-out SUV past another rusted out, boarded up mobile home with as many dogs chained in the front yard as beaters on blocks in the driveway.

It wasn't just the potholes that kept us from riding through here. Merc had borrowed a nondescript, blacked out SUV from where I would never ask. Didn't need to know. My brother had come through like he always did.

"Yeah."

He just shook his head and kept his hand lazy on the pistol in the holster under his shirt.

Lawnmower Jay had been a funny kid we'd gone to school with. Right up until high school when some piece of shit cracked him over the head with a birdhouse he'd made in shop class. Busted up the birdhouse *and* his brain.

Ever since, he lived in his mother's old trailer, with a large shop in the back where he repaired and rebuilt lawnmowers and other small engines. Not that many people out in the desert had lawns to mow.

People, even in the Bends, generally left him alone. I was grateful for that. He didn't deserve more shit from life.

When we pulled in, he stopped what he was doing, stood, and stared at the truck as I put it in park and climbed from the driver's seat. His smile, when he recognized me, was wide and missing at least one tooth since the last time I'd seen him.

"Cam!" His childlike excitement made me feel sick. I didn't deserve his hero worship.

Without our bikes, without our cuts, we were just two more customers for Lawnmower Jay. Two random white guys in peckerwood territory, nothing to see.

"What's up, buddy?" I patted him on his shoulder and gave it a squeeze. I always felt like if I gave too much, I'd spook him—not enough and I'd make him sad.

His smile got wider as he gaped past me at Merc. "Need a mower fixed? I don't do much with bikes, but I do mowers. I'll take care of whatever you need, on the house." He spun and pulled tarps off machines he'd rebuilt—push mowers and ride-ons. His skinny arms tugged hard, and a tarp flapped in the air before falling beside him. "You can have one of these if you want."

Merc gave me a sideways curious glance as Jay walked ahead, rattling off facts about each mower.

"Remember when I got expelled?"

"Beating the shit out of that preppy fuck in the locker room?" Merc dug out the memory.

"Yeah, pretty sure he didn't like birdhouses." Not enough of Jay's mind was gone that he didn't understand what happened to him, who had done it, and what had transpired after.

Merc grunted, putting the correct pieces together, but said nothing more.

"No mowers today, Jay. Wanted to stop by and see how you were doing."

"I'm doing real good." He stopped and smiled at us. "Want a chair? A soda? Ain't got no beer—don't like the way it tastes."

"No, man, we won't be here long. Place looks good." I inspected the area and gestured at the equipment in his shed. "Might need a new cherry picker and toolbox." I'd make it happen, whether he helped me or not.

"Yeah, yeah. Keep meaning to get a new cherry picker, but the chains on this one are still good." They were, but the machine used to heft motors and other things was missing its wheels and hanging onto its last days.

"Seen any Kings lately?"

"Like you or dressed up?" He made a face, like he just realized we weren't in our cuts.

Merc shrugged, giving the front of his t-shirt a tug. "Either."

"I seen Zach, the skinny one with the tattoos on his head. But he lives just over the hill, right before you start in the Bends. I think maybe he has a girlfriend here."

He meant Ghost. Kenna didn't live anywhere close to the Bends, hadn't since she was a kid. David had made sure of that. But I wasn't surprised to hear Ghost had been down here.

Jay made a show of looking around, like someone might pop out of the junk piles next door to eavesdrop. "But there's two that don't dress up. Seen them at the diner wearing their vests, but not here." He lowered his voice. "They come to *Wanda's*. She got a card place in the back now, told me never tell no body bout it when I cut her grass."

When my brows raised, he knew he'd said the right thing and . "They was there today."

Merc caught my gaze, whipped out his phone, and showed him a picture. "One of them, this guy?"

"Yup."

I looked over his shoulder. It was Preacher. Not proof he'd killed Archer, but it was a start.

"If you see them again, can you send me pictures?"

He shifted back and forth on his feet, unsure. "But Wanda and the boys..."

"Will never find out it was you. I promise." I scribbled my number on one of his business cards laying on a mower and handed it to him. Then I counted out five one-hundred-dollar bills and dropped the c-notes onto the seat of one of his rebuilt riding mowers. "Drop that off at Archer's this week, and I'll throw in a few more." With all the rocks and sand, it would just hang out in the garage. But the sale made Jay beam.

He snatched up the money. "I can deliver tomorrow."

"Wait until next week, after you send me pictures."

"I can do that, Cam. I can do that."

We were back at the clubhouse, and I was about to call Riley. She was supposed to meet me here. I got jumpy when she was late. As my phone rang, a number with a familiar prefix appeared on the screen. I answered it, panic momentarily welling in my chest. Why the fuck would the hospital call me unless something had happened to her?

"Mr. Savage?" A woman's clipped, but polite voice filled the line.

"Yes."

"Sir, this is Anna from St. Catherine's Hospital. I'm calling you because you're listed as the Emergency contact for Robbie..."

Everything after that bled into soundless vibration. I understood what the nurse was saying, but it was like someone else listened for me.

The door to the clubhouse swung open and Riley walked in, her eyes adjusting to the dark before landing on me. *What's wrong?* she mouthed as she crossed the distance to me.

"It's Ro, I need to..."

Riley said nothing, just turned back the way she came, held the door open, and then followed me to the bike. Twenty-four hours ago, I'd thought Preacher would strike out at me through Riley.

I'd been wrong. That's not where he hit me. I should have known better.

Twenty-Six

CAM

The steady hums and beeps of the machines in the hospital blended with the murmur of hushed voices until all I heard was a deafening buzz. That sound made me want to jab something sharp into my ears.

Angry, unable to shelve the emotion that threatened to boil over, I paced the long, but mostly empty, hallway. I think the nurse in the ICU took one look at me and knew I'd rip the place apart if I was forced into a waiting room with dozens of people I didn't know. She let me stay.

When I passed the seat Riley perched on, she reached for my hand and gave my fingers a gentle, reassuring squeeze. She was there. I wasn't alone. Knowing that was the only thing that kept me from losing my shit.

"Mr. Savage?" The nurse that approached me was a lanky man with a slight southern drawl. "She's out of surgery and awake. They had to put several pins in, but the arm should heal fine. The orthopedic surgeon will stop by in the morning with a full update. She's not intubated. She's able to breathe on her own, so she should be getting a private room soon. She'll stay here a few days, though, to make sure the concussion heals properly."

He stepped in, leaning close. "I don't know what happened, but...there is a counselor I'd like her to speak to."

I cut my eyes to Riley, then back to him. He was one of those overly friendly and helpful people. They were misguided and well meaning, thinking the system could save women like Ro and my mother. I'd met too many of them to count as a kid.

But Ro wasn't like mom. This had nothing to do with her. It all landed firmly on me. I'd make damn sure it never happened again. I shoved past him, leaving my girl to handle it. And Riley would; she'd smooth everything over so I didn't have to.

There'd been fear on his face. I was a Desert King, the bad guy. He wasn't going to believe anything I had to say, anyway.

In the room, the buzzing sound slid away. It was quiet here, removed from the business of the hospital outside the door that I'd shut softly. If she was asleep, I didn't want to wake her.

One look at Ro and I had to turn away. Her face was swollen, unrecognizable. Her nose, obviously broken, lips busted and scabbed over. I choked on a wave of rage; it stole my breath and the ability to move other than to shake.

When I'd steeled myself to see it again, I turned back to her. Over my life, I'd seen some fucked up shit. But that someone had survived being beaten like that was—

She cracked an eye open and winced. "Can't say you didn't warn me."

Crying wasn't something I was used to. I pressed the heels of my hands against my eyes to staunch the tears and laughed without humor. "Fuck, I wish you'd listened."

"Used to...say the same...about you," she mumbled between thready breaths.

Riley came in then, sliding around me to sit in a chair beside the bed, and thread her fingers through Ro's. That hand seemed to be the only thing not busted or blue.

I moved to the foot of her bed, not trusting myself to go any further. If I did, I'd leave the hospital and track down Preacher. The club be damned. My eyes burned, and I gripped the plastic bedrail and it creaked under the pressure, threatening to crumble.

I'd destroy him for this. No patch or club rule was going to stop me. I'd never wanted to kill a man more. "I never thought he'd go this far."

She sighed. "He needed money. I didn't have it to give him."

"That's not why he did this." Looking at her hurt, so I cast my gaze to Riley.

Ro shook her head, grunting in pain as she did. "It is. He thought Archer hid it at my place. Tried to force me to tell him where it was."

Riley shot a frantic glance at me. I shook my head no. We weren't even telling Ro. I willed her to see the conviction in my eyes. If he had done this to Ro thinking she knew, he'd do worse to Riley if he found out she had the money.

"I talked to the lawyer. There isn't a huge sum of cash. Mostly, just properties like your place and the house." Riley's voice was cool and convincing. Lying like that, she'd make one hell of a lawyer.

"I know him," Ro garbled, like she was talking through a mouth full of broken glass. "He believes there's money and won't stop until he finds it."

She cast her open eye at Riley. A lot can be said with a look, even one from a woman with a face busted all to hell. Everything about the way she watched Riley was a warning similar to the one I'd given.

He'd never get that close to Riley. I'd kill him first and smile all the way to prison, saying *cheese motherfucker* for my mugshot.

"He owes somebody." Her lips pulled apart, and she winced again. "Yeah."

"Pretty sure we know who," I said, then blew out a hard breath.

***

I was outside the emergency room doors, smoking, but every inch of me wanted to be at the clubhouse killing Preacher. Riley was the only reason I wasn't. She'd convinced me to stay until Ro was settled in her room, asleep.

And she'd be safe here. I'd already called Deputy Wyatt and made sure there would be someone keeping an eye on her, even when I couldn't. Not that I expected Preacher to be that bold. He was waiting on me to react.

Riley came out the doors and scanned the parking deck until she saw me. Then her mouth settled in a relieved half smile. Like she'd thought I'd left, road out, and done exactly what I'd wanted to do.

Her pouty upper lip flirted with me even now. Made me want to kiss her stupid and find a different way to blow off some steam. The monster that raged inside me turned, took one look at her, and wanted her, too. And that's why Riley was different from every other woman. The whole of me, even the bad parts, wanted her.

Only she could tame the beast.

"Hey." She wrapped her arms around my middle and snuggled in like she knew I was barely hanging on; that I needed her to keep from collapsing into the darkness.

I flicked the cigarette butt into the outdoor ashtray and kissed her hair, inhaling the clean scent of her.

There were moments when it wasn't about sex, when touching her was about something more. Riley was comfort, she provided a soothing security I'd never felt from anyone else. Here, with her, was my safe space.

I could never thank her enough for that. Never repay that debt. But I could protect her, get her the fuck out of Hayes County, and away from Preacher. And never had I wanted to do that more than right then.

"I know I'm not supposed to know things, and you can't tell me anything. But I met Garza, spoke to him."

She was right on the money with that. It was Garza who'd scared Preacher so badly he'd beaten Ro nearly to death. There were bylaws, a code that all of us wearing the cut had to abide by. Riley was right about that, too. The very same code that saved my life had killed Archer.

I was beginning to wonder if it was worth it anymore.

"I don't know what Preacher got himself into, but it ain't just gambling. Whatever it is, it's more than that." The words kept coming when they shouldn't. "Garza showing up at the fight like that was a statement. He'll come for the MC next. This ball is rolling now, Riley. I don't know if I can stop it."

I kissed her on the top of the head and pulled back, dragging her to the bike. "But I can sure as fuck keep you safe."

Twenty-Seven

RILEY

Even in his stillness there was a jumpy edge to Cam, like he teetered on the brink of something deadly and dangerous. I'd sat across from Val Soletsky, read the danger there. But it had been cool, calculated. This was the opposite. Cam Savage was a land mine just waiting for someone to step on him. I'd witnessed what he could do when in this state.

I was pretty sure he was praying the person who set him off was Preacher.

"Hey." I placed a hand on his shoulder. The tension there radiated all the way up my arm.

It was full dark now, and only the light from the driveway filtered through the blinds into the living room of his apartment. We weren't staying in the house, too many entry points. I'd never imagined living a life where I'd be concerned about things like that. It should have scared me more than it did.

But even after what happened to Ro, I wasn't afraid. Because Cam was with me and with him close, no one could hurt me.

He turned, pulled me in, and cradled me in his arms, nuzzling his face against the side of my hair. He trembled once as I clung to him. It was like he needed me to stand there to ground himself, to remind him of who we were.

"What can I do?" I asked softly.

"Nothing." He sighed, rubbing his hands over my back.

I slipped my arms beneath his leather vest and wrapped them tight around his middle.

"I know you want to stay," he breathed the words against my hair, almost in a whisper.

"But you're afraid I'll get hurt if I do." I leaned back to look at him in the semi-darkness. "Cam, I won't go without you."

His response was a kiss. A slow, methodical one, like he was memorizing the shape of my lips, the caress of my tongue. This kiss was a sensual slide into warm arousal. His hands slipped beneath my shirt, rough against my skin, as he guided me backward to the table in the corner of the room.

"Take everything off," he said, then his tongue rasped down my neck.

I did as I was told, ditching everything as he did the same. We moved in silence. The only sounds were the swish of cloth sliding to the floor, then the clang and thud of metal and leather when Cam tossed his vest to the chair.

He laid me back on that table. The top was cool against my back, and he lifted my knees, spreading my legs. He started at my ankle, lifting and cradling it and placing kisses there, then up the inside of my legs, and further still, until he kissed my pussy.

I closed my eyes, clung to his hair, and let the pleasure wash over me. He traced the line of my sex with his tongue, needing no light to navigate. His tongue dipped in and back out before being replaced by two warm fingers as he flicked upward to my clit. He moaned, the vibration erotic and sexy, and made me squirm.

My breath caught as the friction built when he stretched and turned his fingers, stroking that magical place inside me. That secret place that only he'd ever found. Crying out in the darkness, I trembled with aftershocks as he pulled me up, kissing me.

He picked me up, carried me across the room, and fell back on the couch, pulling me across him so that I straddled his lap. "I want you like this."

I made a face, and he laughed. "We're re-christening it, darlin'."

The momentary spark of nervous energy was washed away when his arousal brushed against my slit. "And I want to see you."

He reached over and flicked open the blinds so that the moonlight filtered in.

Beneath me, his hair messy, his lips shining, and his eyes heavy, Cam Savage was the sexiest thing I'd ever seen. He stole my breath, made my heart beat fast, and warmed me all over.

Caught in his sleepy blue gaze, I guided him to my entrance with trembling fingers, then slid slowly down the length of him.

He rubbed his lips together and sucked in a breath. Moving slowly at first, I rocked my hips, then rose up and sank back down, my hands braced on Cam's chest.

His muscles were rigid, his body tight as he gripped my hips. The faster I moved, the harder he clung to me. Then he dragged his fingers up my sides, around to my breasts, cupping them and squeezing them.

"You're beautiful," he murmured.

When I found a rhythm that felt good, that sent goose flesh over my skin, Cam groaned louder. I kept that steady up, then down, grinding my hips as I went, until another orgasm rocked through me.

I brought my hands to Cam's, covering his over my breasts, and glanced down to watch his head roll back and his eyes squeeze shut, his hips bucking beneath me.

He was much more than just beautiful right then. He was everything. He was mine.

It was in that moment I knew that no matter what happened, no one was going to take him from me.

***

The sound of bikes woke us both. My head on his chest, Cam's heart instantly thundered as if he'd been shot. He moved me gently, sat up, and pulled on his jeans before snatching up the pistol and flicking off the safety.

"Stay back here."

I ignored his gruff command.

It wasn't just the sound of one bike, but of many. Fear screamed that it was the entire club, that they were coming for him. Preacher had told them God knows what. Now Cam was done.

Fresh, hot tears threatened as I jerked on his t-shirt and followed him through the small living room. He pulled the blinds down before shooting me a sideways glance.

"Do you ever listen?"

"Not really, no." I was shaking, but not from cold.

He kissed me once, firmly. "I mean it, don't follow me out. Whatever happens, today or tomorrow or whenever, if I can't get to you...go with Merc, okay? He'll take care of you."

"Wait, what?" I grabbed his free hand and tugged on it.

He stilled at the door as the sound of bike engines shut off below us.

"Trust me, okay? I'll keep you safe."

He shook me off and slipped out the door. I didn't listen, of course, and peeked through the crack where he didn't shut it all the way. He stood at the railing, gun behind his back. Below him, Merc slipped off his bike.

I knew every face. Merc. Puck. Jester. Dekes. AP.

The gang's all here. Well, most of them.

Merc lifted both hands, palms up, but said nothing. Jester and Puck ambled toward the table under the carport. "You said I'd know when it's time. Brother, it's time."

Cam visibly relaxed, his shoulders dropping and bringing his hand around. He turned to me, swore under his breath, and kissed me once. "Go back to bed. I'll be up later."

What he meant was that he was safe, but I couldn't be a part of whatever this was. I should be mad about that, but I had my own secrets.

"I'm going to go through some of Archer's stuff. I can't just sit up here, worried."

He waited for me to pull on some soft pants before walking down the stairs. They all convened around the table at the carport. I didn't bother with a greeting, just scooted by them all, unlocked Archer's backdoor, and went inside.

Unlike Preacher when he'd tossed the house, I knew what I was looking for. But I couldn't remember in which box of mementoes I'd stashed it. Every so often, I glanced out a window to check on Cam. I could hear voices but couldn't make out the words. The only thing I could really see in the darkness was the occasional flicker of light from burning embers as various men smoked. No shouting, no fast movements...Cam was safe.

Rifling through a large, masculine jewelry box, I hit pay-dirt. Nestled amidst the large rings and leather bands was a piece of lavender paper. A woman's lipstick pressed against it, a phone number, and a woman's name.

Sasha.

Twenty-Eight

CAM

"How is she?" AP pulled a chair out and lowered himself to it with a groan, wincing as he sat.

"Should be asking you about that." I lit a cigarette and leaned against one of the support posts. I couldn't sit, not now.

"I'm old as fuck, son. Haven't slept in days, and my back's screwed to shit until I get to the chiropractor."

Jester pulled a bottle from his pocket, shook out a pill, and passed it to him. "To cure what ails you."

AP popped the pain pill into his mouth and chewed it for faster relief. I flinched. I couldn't do it. I hated those things. The loss of control wasn't for me. That's why I never did more than drink and smoke a little weed.

Dekes leaned back in another chair, steepling his fingers on his chest. "You ain't going Nomad, kid. I ain't about to let it happen. We need you here."

"Not much choice. I can't sit at a table with him."

"Brother." Dekes sighed. "He's not going to let you do that."

"Shouldn't be his choice. It's a table vote."

"I don't know if I can." This from AP. "It sets a precedent, Cam. If you wear the hooligan patch; that's heavy."

The rest of them hung their heads and stayed quiet. Once you'd killed for the Kings, they owned you. I'd earned that patch a long time ago. Before Riley, before I thought of a life without the club. There were other options, though.

I hadn't allowed myself to think about those, to think what it could mean. Not really, but now I needed to. We all did.

"I can't do this without you." Merc spoke up first, from the other side of the carport.

"It wouldn't be forever, just while he's at the head of the table."

"We can change that in a few months." This from Puck.

Only the four of us knew. Telling the rest of them my suspicions could create a vacuum that would suck up the entire club, then spit it out dirty and broken.

"I can't be in the same charter as him, regardless." Because of what I knew. "I'm out, with the patch or without it."

Dekes closed his eyes tight. Merc swore, but didn't look shocked.

"The fuck?" Jester was the most surprised. "What did he do that was so bad you're gonna do that to yourself? Jesus fucking Christ, Savage."

"I've known Archer my whole god-damn life." AP rubbed a hand over his tired, haggard face. "Ain't no way he shot himself."

Panic swelled in my chest. I hadn't said it, wouldn't, but I sure as fuck believed Preacher had killed Archer. Now I knew why. And that was something I couldn't tell anyone. A secret I'd take to my grave to protect Riley.

"He's got himself into some shit with Garza." I said it low. "It's why they showed up last night, why he's pushing the peckerwoods so hard."

"And he's been with Wanda a lot lately." Merc said before I could. "Then beat the shit out of Ro to bait Cam into doing something stupid. Because he thinks he's the only one who knows."

"You're all your own men." AP cut in. "Can make your own decisions. But whatever is going on, Archer knew. He talked to me before he died. Was looking for a way to get Preach out, before it blew back on the rest of us."

That bomb hit and exploded everything I'd ever known, or thought I'd known. AP leveled a hard gaze at me, and I knew that he knew. About the money. About the cartel. About all of it. He was just waiting for us to put it together.

For the same reason I hadn't brought it to the guys, he hadn't either.

"This affects more than just the table."

"And he's got a lot of friends." This from Puck, who broke out a bag and started to roll a joint. "Even if we could prove it, I don't know how we'd convince everyone."

"But if Cam goes after him for Ro, he's going to spin it." Merc again.

"He thought Ro knew where Archer hid a bunch of cash." I rubbed that itch at the back of my neck, straightened, and pulled my cigarettes from my pocket. "I don't think he was just after me, but he's running scared."

"Can we find out what the cartel wants from him?" Dekes asked.

Jester snorted. "Brother, you wanna go ask Garza? Be my guest. Because he's going to hold us all accountable."

He was right. No use kicking up that hornet's nest until we could hand him Preacher. But none of it mattered, because I was done. I had to be. I thought of Ro, of how beaten and broken she was. We had the money. Preacher at least believed we did. Riley wasn't safe, wouldn't be, as long as we stayed.

I'd take that beating a thousand times over to keep Riley safe.

"I'm out of time." I sighed, took a drag from my cigarette, and flicked the ashes. "If he thinks there's money, he thinks Riley has it. I've got to get her out of here. Only two ways that happens."

"Nomad or we take the patch." Dekes agreed now, nodding his head solemnly. "Love is a big thing, brother. Never forget that."

"Fuck." Jester jumped up and stormed off.

I understood that sentiment. Felt it down in my bones.

Twenty-Nine

Riley

Standing at the bedroom window for what felt like the thirtieth time, I glanced out beneath the carport. The conversation wasn't heated, but there was passion in it. These men, brothers, loved Cam and he them.

If I could do anything to save him from leaving this life he loved, I would. And I'd do more to keep him whole and alive.

I moved to the couch, curling on it as one after another the sound of rumbling Harleys motored down the driveway and out into the night. Merc stayed awhile, standing near his bike, talking to Cam. I could make out their voices, but not the words, again.

The sound of the two of them together comforted me until I dozed off.

Cam, bathed in the light from the kitchen, sat on the couch and pulled my legs onto his lap. His face was stoic and looked as if he'd aged ten years in those few hours.

I sat up, crawling onto his lap, cuddling him, as the sound of Merc's bike disappeared.

"Can you go check on Ro for me tomorrow? Then hang out at Dylan's until I come get you?"

"Why? What's happening?"

He exhaled a deep sigh. "You know I can't tell you that."

"Then tell me what you can." I couldn't tell if I shivered from fear or cold.

"Chapel tomorrow. There are rules, bylaws that bind us to the MC. Preacher broke the biggest one, but I can't prove it. So, I'm going Nomad." He stood, cradling me for a few long minutes, then let my legs drop to the floor. "Like I told you before, we start a new life. I keep the patch but not a charter."

I followed him out of the house and upstairs to his apartment.

"Is Sasha the prostitute my dad used?" I asked as he shucked his pants, and I climbed into bed with him, snuggling against the warmth of his chest.

He seemed to think. "I'll be honest. I don't remember her name. But yeah, sounds right. Why?"

"I saw her at the motel, too. If he was there meeting her, maybe she saw Preacher?"

Cam sighed. "Even if she did, darlin', Val's never going to let her talk. It's bad for his business."

"It's murder, I'm sure—"

"Next, you're going to tell me Val's some great guy who would care about that. Because he was nice to you. He's a mobster. He does worse daily."

"It won't hurt anything for me to call her, to ask, will it?"

He kissed me gently. "If you want to, go for it. But don't get your hopes up."

"If I can convince her to tell them, then you don't have to go Nomad."

He chuckled. "I love you."

"I love you, too." And that's exactly why I had to try.

"After tomorrow, it's over, one way or another. Let's get some sleep."

I didn't. I counted the minutes and his breathing until the sun came up.

***

When Cam left me that morning, there was a giant cloud of dread that lingered in his wake like phantom exhaust. Maybe it was the lack of sleep that made things feel so heavy, so out of my control. Or maybe it was the way he'd kissed me like it was the last time, like he was memorizing every inch of my lips.

I got dressed in jeans, a black tank top, and black boots. Like I was going to battle instead of off to see Ro at the hospital like I said I would.

She was sitting up in her bed, the television on, and the room smelled like stale cafeteria food. Her broken smile tugged at her swollen, scabbed lips, and made me inwardly cringe. I kept my feelings buried and tried to look happy to see her.

When really, I wanted to be at the clubhouse, to know what was happening with Cam.

"Cam wanted me to swing by and check on you." I took her hand and sat.

I was used to looking at the sickly shell of a person. But this was different, though in pain, Ro was still Ro. Just a bloodied, swollen version. She squeezed my hand.

"He won't be back here. Pretty sure I'll never see him again."

"No." My heart ached for her. "No, I don't think so. He's not angry, not at you."

"Oh, he was." She laughed without humor. "And he was right."

"I'm so sorry, Ro."

"Not your fault, sweet girl. This was all me."

But it wasn't. Nothing gave Preacher the right to hurt her like this, to hurt anyone like this. There were differences. Cam had hurt people, but never someone innocent, never someone that couldn't fight back or hadn't done something worse. "I'm worried. They're about to go to Chapel."

She breathed out a rattling breath. "They'll kill each other."

"That's what I'm afraid of." I closed my eyes tight against the emotion. She'd put words to my biggest fear. Tears ran hot down my cheeks, unchecked.

"You might be Archer's girl, but you're your mama's daughter. Don't forget that. She took no shit. I remember."

That made me chuckle in spite of my fear. She wasn't wrong. "You're right."

"Don't let him shut you out. Don't be like me, have a voice. Use it."

I still had Sasha's number in my pocket. It tingled there. I stayed with Ro for more than an hour until her pain meds kicked in and she slept. I left with a key to her place to pick up some clothes and feed her cat.

In my car, I dialed the number. A sleepy, accented woman's voice answered on the third ring. "Hi, Sasha. This is Riley Bowman. Archer's daughter—"

There was a hesitation. "I'm so sorry, but I can't help you," she said with remorse clear in her voice

"Please listen." I willed her not to hang up, to hear me out, convinced I could make her see things my way. "I know this is scary." I took a steadying breath. "Have you ever been in love? To the point you'd do anything to save the man you love? Even if it meant sacrificing everything?"

She didn't respond but remained on the line. I could hear the faint sound of music behind her, like she was driving.

"We know Preacher killed my father. Just like I know you were there with Archer that night. I just need proof for Cam."

"I cannot help you." She enunciated carefully. "But you called the wrong person. You should try speaking with Val."

The exact thing Cam didn't think would matter.

I tried calling the club and had to leave a message, because, of course, he wasn't in. Maybe Cam was right.

Thirty

CAM

At this point, I knew everything I needed to. Preacher had pushed too far. He wanted me to snap, and I'd come damn close.

I closed my eyes for a moment on an open stretch of deserted highway, tossing my hands out wide in a fucked-up game of chicken I played every so often since I'd got my first bike.

One...two...three...

Then Riley, naked and moving above me, flashed through my mind, and I opened my eyes, dropped my arms back to the handlebars, and kicked the throttle up a notch. The nerves that twisted in my gut weren't as strong as the image of her, the memory of the feel of her.

God, I'd never loved anything as much as I did her. Not even the fucking Desert Kings.

Of the current table, only two weren't with me. Drop Top, who would remain neutral in all club business until the day he died, and Paul.

The rest were mine. And Ivan and his crew were on the way in as backup.

No, I wasn't going to accuse Preacher of murdering Archer. My gut instinct wasn't proof enough.

The decision had been made. I was leaving the club. And if he wouldn't let me go Nomad, this was the last time I'd ride this bike. Maybe the last time I'd ride at all. Preacher wouldn't let them take it easy on me.

Skin for the patch. They didn't just take the leather, they took it out of me. A beat down, one that would leave me looking worse than Ro. I didn't fear that, if it meant Riley was safe. To be honest with myself, I had never feared pain. Even before her.

I took the long way around, through the hills and past the rock formations. The midday sun had warmed my leather as I pulled into the clubhouse. I was resolute in my decision. Riley's safety, a life with her, was more important than anything else.

Archer had known that. I knew now why he'd brought her here to me.

To get me out.

Everyone was there. Merc and AP waiting outside the clubhouse door, Ivan's entire table milling around the parking lot, cutting up with Puck and the others.

"This what you really want?" over his bald head as I climbed off the bike.

He meant the Nomad vote. As it would take another president to make that happen, a second voice to agree to let me ride wherever I wanted with no accounting. No charter to answer to.

"Yup."

He gripped my arm, forcing me to look at him. Ivan was only a few years older than me and had been in the club since he was old enough to ride. He bled Desert King gold. But he was a friend. "You better be damn sure, because I don't think the old guy's gonna budge."

And Preacher would have to. As president, he could veto any vote. Even this one.

"Then I've got one other option," I said with solemn honesty.

Ivan balked, his skin going pale and his eyes widening in something adjacent to fear. "Cam, bro, that's—"

"What will probably happen," Merc finished for him, tossed the cigarette he'd been smoking to the ground, and crushed it out with his boot. "Ain't no way Preacher is letting him go. Not like this."

Not when I had something he wanted.

"Jesus, man. There are other ways."

I knew what ways he meant. "Absolutely fucking not. He won't touch her; I'll kill him first." The anger that flashed through me could have set me on fire. There were club rules. I wanted out, I could get beat out—my arms broken, give them my bike. Or let Preacher fuck Riley.

Never. Fucking. Happen.

"It's a button he'll push," Ivan whispered, so that only I heard him. He'd made it obvious he'd never been Preacher's biggest fan.

I just shrugged, jerked open the door, and strolled in. This early, none of the pass-arounds were here, but some of the patches had heard rumors of shit. They milled about the clubhouse waiting on shit to hit the fan.

followed me through, while Ivan and his crew took up residence just outside the hallway.

Preacher was there, sitting at the head of the table like a proud father. As if he'd done something worthy, other than beat a woman to within an inch of her life. I hadn't been fully prepared to see him.

Rage ripped through me like molten iron, scorching everything in its path until the corners of my vision blurred red.

I glared at him, willing him to say something, anything.

But I wasn't the one who had called the meeting. We'd decided that last night, so he ignored me and turned his attention to AP.

"What's up?"

"I think you know," AP sat beside him, the air in the room as heavy as his sigh.

Preacher made an innocent gesture with his hands palm up. "The MC can't get involved in a domestic altercation."

"She's my godmother, Preach," I said through gritted teeth.

"Not my problem," he pointed out.

Rage coiled violently in my gut, ready to strike.

"Except that it is," AP responded quietly, drawing his line in the sand.

Preacher, for the first time, realized he'd overstepped. The smugness evaporated from his face and he sat straighter. "We got drunk, she got mouthy, and things got out of control," he said slowly, as if that made it all better.

This was the plan: Use what happened to Ro to let me go Nomad. AP's idea. He figured it would keep the drama as low as possible. And when I could prove Preacher had a hand in Archer's death, we'd handle the rest.

Or we'd ditch him in the annual vote in a few months. Either way, getting me the fuck out of here was the best option for the club.

For Riley.

But every word Preacher said about Ro pulled me tighter than a bowstring.

"Fuck, did she talk to the cops?" Drop Top rubbed a hand through his beard. "The sheriff won't look past a domestic violence case, not even for us."

I caught Merc's gaze and held it.

"Pay the hospital, toss her some cash." This from Paul.

Dekes, Puck, Jester, and Merc didn't say a word.

Preacher shrugged. "That why we're here? To appease the kid so he minds his own fucking business?"

"How about you learn to keep your fucking hands off women?" I shot back, annoyed. "Stop being a little bitch when you can't win an argument."

"We going down this road again, *boy*?"

I shook my head and pursed my lips. "Nah, Preach. No roads, not with you. I want Nomad. I'd rather rock by myself than stick around with a pussy who beats women."

He laughed, relaxing back in his chair. "Kid, you know too damn much."

"Cam wouldn't tell shit," Merc said simply. "Put it to a vote."

"Explains why White Pine is down today." Preacher huffed. But his brain was turning, like he couldn't quite figure out why I'd want to go Nomad. "Lone Wolf ain't going to keep her safe, kid. Archer's enemies are still out there."

"Even the one who killed him." His veiled threat to Riley's life nearly pushed me over the edge. I crossed my arms over my chest, let my right hand rest on the nine-millimeter resting there.

I'd blow his god-damned head off. Right here at this table.

He caught my gaze, held it, but gave away nothing save the few beads of sweat that formed across the wrinkle on his forehead. "Archer's demons killed him."

"They sure the fuck did. He should have left them in the desert." I never blinked.

He looked away first. "I'm about done with this shit. You got something to say, fucking say it, Savage."

"Take the vote," I responded cooly.

You could tell he didn't want to and judging how his eyes narrowed, the answer was no. I'd steeled myself for this, been ready for it.

"Where you gonna go, riding Nomad?" He leaned forward. "Without the club, you got no job, no house. Gonna sell little miss sunshine's ass?"

I ignored the dig and smiled. "Archer took care of his kid, brother. She ain't gonna have to *sell shit*."

I regretted the words the instant I said them. I let him push me, let him push me too far. A flash of knowledge lit in his eyes. He interpreted my words correctly, knew there was money, and the fucker knew I had it.

I'd rather his attention be on me than on her, anyway. I cocked my head to one side and curved my mouth in a half smile of sarcastic challenge. *Try me, mother fucker.*

"Call for the vote, Preacher." This from Drop Top, annoyed that any of this was happening at all.

"Yay or nay for Savage to go Nomad." He looked around the table. "Nay."

Then to me next. "Yeah."

Puck. "Whatever he wants, yay."

Dekes. "Yay. But I fucking hate it."

Paul, who glanced nervously around to Preacher. "Nay." But it sounded half like a question.

Then to Jester. "If it's what he wants, yay."

Merc, who cut a slow dangerous gaze to Preacher, knowing as well as I did the old man was going to veto it. "Ivan is waiting. Going this far, I'm all in. Yes."

AP, eyes aimed at the table. "Yay."

Preacher twisted the gavel for a while. "All this bullshit, the peckerwoods, Archer dying, I feel like you're trying to tear down everything we've built here at every turn. I can't trust you to stay loyal without Archer to keep you in line. Veto." He cracked the gavel onto the table.

AP and Merc's gazes lifted to me. Merc's mouth tightened, and he gripped the edge of the table, gently shaking his head no.

But like I'd told him last night on Archer's patio. Preacher wasn't going to stop, not until he took everything from me, because I was the only one who knew. And he wanted something from Riley and even if he got it, he'd kill her.

I wasn't about to let that happen. This ended here, today.

"If this is who we are now, I want none of it." I stood, shrugged the cut off my shoulders, and tossed it to the table. "Fuck you, Preacher."

He didn't even hide the gleeful turn of his lips. "You're really going to do this?"

I laughed without humor. He had no clue how far I'd go.

"Once it's done, there aren't any more bylaws between us, Preacher. Gear up to fucking run."

The room ran ice cold as I left. The weight I'd carried since Archer's death was gone. I could handle the pain. To keep her safe, I'd take it over and over.

To protect Riley, I'd do whatever it fucking took.

As the door shut behind me, a bomb went off. I couldn't tell who shouted the loudest, but Preacher had lost the table.

I'd lost my club.

Ivan stood, took a good look at me, and lowered himself back into his seat, his face sick. "Jesus, Cam."

Merc was right on my heels. "I'm not doing it." His voice hard.

"You have to."

"The hell with that." He was prepared to argue when AP walked out and clamped a firm hand on his shoulder.

"We all signed up for this, kid."

"Well, I'm gonna need a god-damned hour or two." He turned back to Preacher, who stood in the doorway to chapel. "You hear me?"

"Do what you have to do."

And I knew what that was. It made me sick to think of Merc going down that path again, taking those chances. Addiction was real. But I don't think I could do to him what I was asking him to do to me sober. I ducked my head as he walked out.

Jester with him, tossing an arm over his shoulder as they strolled out the side doors.

Thirty-One

RILEY

I pulled into Dylan's driveway still reeling from the conversation with Sasha. Angry, too, that I couldn't get in touch with Val. I realized it was entitled to think he had the time to talk to me. But this right now consumed every part of my life.

Cam hadn't answered my phone call either.

I'd been so lost in my thoughts I didn't notice Dylan in the driveway, tears rolling down her face, and shouting. I hopped out of the car to see her shaking a bag in Merc's face, while he sat astride his bike.

"Hey, what's wrong?" Fear arced through me, making me walk faster. Had something happened to Cam?

She spun on me, her pretty blue eyes caught somewhere between disbelief and accusation. "He's out. That selfish little fuck would rather send my brother back to hell than grow some god-damned balls."

"*Dylan*." Merc's face was hard, his eyes sad, but the warning in his voice was crystal clear. "Stop."

Relief flooded through me. I'd been envisioning Cam killing Preacher, blowing the whole club up, or worse. I approached them on unsteady feet. "But that's good, right? It's over now. He's Nomad, we can go. This can—"

She looked at me as if she might actually hit me, then shook her head. "You honestly think he could just leave? Nomad isn't a real option for Cam. He's—there are things he's done, things he knows, that can never leave Dry Valley. If he goes, he's out. And if he's out..." Her voice was shrill, and she glared at her brother.

Judging by her panic, there were things he hadn't told me. "Explain."

"Yeah, Merc. Tell her why you were about to shoot up. How you just chased me all the way back to the house to get your smack back." She shook the baggy at him again.

He closed his eyes, leaned against her Jeep, and sighed heavily. "You know why I wanted to do it, Dyl. I can't." Angst stole his words.

She rounded on me, not crying now, her eyes wide and angry. "There are only two ways out, Riley. Skin or ass. He's not going to let Preacher fuck you, which means they are going to hurt him, hurt him bad. He won't ride again, won't be whole. He'll be lucky if he survives. It's a bunch of barbaric bullshit for no god-damned reason."

My whole world spun, and I wobbled unsteadily on my feet. Merc moved, taking me by the elbows and lowering me to the concrete. Vomit rushed up the back of my throat, I choked on it, and swallowed. I was hot, so very hot, it .

My vision wavered, focusing in and out as blood seemed to rush out of my body.

Then Dylan was there, on her knees in front of me, pulling my hands in front of her and looked to be speaking in soft, gentle tones that I couldn't hear, but her lips seemed to move softer than they had before.

Sound rushed in and I knew what I had to do. I knew a way I could get to Val. I was smart. I listened when nobody knew I was there.

"Merc, I need a favor." I inhaled a deep breath, drinking air in like I'd been starved of it.

"What's that?" He knelt.

"I need to talk to Val Soletsky."

When Merc made a face, I jumped forward and grabbed the front of his vest. "I'm serious. One of his girls was there the night Archer died. I know she was. I just need him to tell her she can talk to me."

He thought about it for a while. "Fuck, I don't have shit else to go on. I hope you've got a fucking Ace of Spades up your ass."

I tried Cam again and prepared myself for the argument coming. I was oddly relieved when he didn't answer.

"Can you buy me some time?" I asked Dylan as Merc climbed on his bike and fired it up.

Her jaw was set in a defiant, determined tilt. "You're damn right I can."

"He's going to beat my ass for this, but climb on." He jerked his chin toward the back of his bike.

"If it helps, he told me if anything happens...to stick close to you."

"It does."

***

Riding behind Merc was very different than riding with Cam. It wasn't just the rider, either. I sat lower on the back of his bike, forced to look around him to see anything. Anxious, I alternated between checking my phone for Cam and craning my neck around Merc's shoulder.

To his credit, he drove fast. We made it to The Black Cat by midafternoon.

The club was already in full swing. When I'd first seen Merc at Dylan's, he'd looked angry and defeated. Now, hope lit his handsome features as he swung his leg off the bike.

I spilled out my plan quickly as we walked to the back entrance. The more I talked, the bigger Merc smiled. "You are *definitely* Archer's daughter."

"I'm figuring that out." I shifted my bag nervously as he talked to the guy at the door. The tiny leather backpack was heavier than ever before. If this worked, I'd be signing Preacher's death warrant. If it didn't, I'd still kill him.

Would I pull the trigger for Cam? *Hell yes.*

The Black Cat wasn't as busy as it had been the last time I was here. Of that, I was thankful. Only a few patrons were scattered about the club. Most were at tables with a dancer perched on their lap, but a few were at the main stage as a girl with long red hair spun lazily on a pole.

Val stood at the end of a hallway, watching the dance. His brow was furrowed, like he was annoyed. He turned to us, saw me, and smiled. "Riley." He walked to me, kissed both of my cheeks, then shook Merc's hand. "What can I do for you?" He asked him more than me.

Merc cocked his chin in my direction. "She's the one that wanted to see you."

The Ukrainian contemplated me for a long time.

Nervous under his inspection, I shifted from foot to foot. "I left a message before I had Merc bring me."

He snorted a laugh. "I'll probably never see it." He nodded me into his office. Judging by the way his employees watched me, this was an unusual move.

This wasn't the sort of place you just showed up out of nowhere. There had to be a reason. I was hoping mine was good enough.

I perched on the edge of the leather chair in front of Val's desk as he shut the door behind Merc and then sat across from me, waiting for me to say something. I'd never imagined a mobster would put me at ease, but the gentle way he watched me did.

"Cam doesn't know I'm here."

"I assumed as much when you showed up here with Merc."

"Listen, I don't know how much I'm supposed to know, and I'm sure I shouldn't be telling you any of it..." I glanced back to Merc, who just shrugged like none of it would matter, anyway.

I clasped my hands in my lap and sighed big. "There's a snake in the Kings. And if I don't flush it out for Cam, I'm afraid my father won't be the only dead biker in Hayes County." The words came out in a rush.

"And what does that have to do with me and my business?"

"My father was close to one of your ladies." I didn't say which, not yet, no reason to get her in trouble. "And I need her to tell me what she saw the night he died."

I caught Val's gaze and didn't back down. This was important.

He steepled his fingers under his chin. "Your father was a very good customer, Riley. I won't lie to you about that. But my job is to protect the women who work for me. I hope you understand. I would never advise one of mine to speak to you."

A lead weight sank in my gut. But I had expected this. I thought about the forlorn look in her eyes. "You're afraid of what the club might do."

"I fear nothing. But angering the Desert Kings is bad for business. I'm sure Cam would say the same about me."

"The only thing that would piss Cam off," I stopped and grinned. "Is me being here without telling him."

"You've got nothing to fear from the Kings." This came from Merc, who lounged against the wall in the corner. "To be honest, you'd be doing us a favor."

"That official?" He raised one elegant eyebrow.

"It is."

"What would Preacher think about that?"

"Dead men don't have opinions." Merc shrugged lazily.

I took a breath, deciding to risk it on Val. I didn't want to lose Cam, but the closer we got to the truth, the scarier Preacher became. "We know Preacher shot Archer. I just need proof."

"Are you sure? Is Savage worth it?"

"Absolutely." I shoved the card I had with Ro's address across the table.

He looked at Merc again. "This have anything to do with the cartel?"

"Probably."

"Being on Garza's good side is good for business."

"Will you be there with Sasha?" I asked him.

He barked something short, quick, and Ukrainian. A door at the back of the room opened and Sasha, in a pair of leggings and an oversized shirt, stepped out.

"I told him you were tenacious."

I stood and hugged her before I could stop myself. "Thank you."

"He was a good man."

Thirty-Two

Riley

My in the parking lot of The Black Cat. I didn't need to look to know it was Cam.

"Hey." I couldn't keep the relief from that one word.

"Where are you?" Cam sounded...broken.

My heart slammed against my chest. "Fixing this."

"It's too late, darlin'. I came by Dylan's to see you, before..." His voice trailed off.

"I'm on my way right now, Cam."

Merc mouthed *ten minutes*.

"I can be there in ten."

"I'm on my way to the clubhouse."

"No. Just wait. I have proof."

But he wasn't listening. Either the phone was cutting out or he was beyond belief. "I love you, darlin'. No matter what happens today, know I've loved you more than anyone in my whole fucking life."

"I love you too. So much." I was crying. Merc climbed on the bike, waiting on me before he fired it up.

I wanted to shout at Cam to run, to get a head start, let Merc and me finish this. But I knew him well enough to know he wasn't the running kind.

"He's going to the clubhouse," I told Merc as I frantically climbed on behind him, fastening the helmet as he tore out.

The ride was fast, stealing my breath and my stomach. I didn't trust Merc like I did Cam. I didn't have that much faith in *anyone*. But he got me to the clubhouse in one piece and didn't leave me enough time to panic.

"You ready?" he asked, hopping off before me and holding his hand out so I could hop off.

I slipped my bag around and off my shoulders, clutching it in one hand. "Yeah."

"Merc!" A biker I didn't know stuck his head out the front door. "They're starting, bro."

He took off around the side of the building. I gave chase, struggling to stay with him, panic making me breathe harder—scared.

I rounded the corner in time to see Jester throw a right so hard, Cam's entire body turned with it, blood flying from his mouth. I screamed, but there was no sound, or if there was, I couldn't hear it.

Everything happened fast. Standing in a circle of doom around Cam, they all turned, Cam looking up, swiping at his mouth, his face contorted with confusion. Preacher barked orders, gesturing at me and jabbing a finger in the air. These were his brothers, his friends, and the brutality of what was happening was almost too much for me to stomach.

Anger surged through me.

A man I didn't recognize charged forward, reaching for me. Merc in front of me, intercepting him. I couldn't hear him, much like everything else, but his smile was mean and far from happy. Whatever he said shocked the other guy enough he backed down and looked toward Preacher for help.

When no one else came for me, I closed my distance on the group, and Preacher charged toward me himself.

I pulled my father's gun, let my leather backpack drop and stepped over it. A forty-five was large and heavy, but my hands didn't tremble as I slid the safety off—a round already chambered.

"One more step and I'll fucking kill you." And I meant every word.

"Baby." Cam was behind me, nuzzling my hair, pulling me against his chest, hand snaking down my arm toward the pistol. "You can't be here."

There was a pain in his voice that would haunt me the rest of my life.

But so would the look on his face when I jerked away to the side closest to Merc. I only hazarded him the quickest glance, but Cam's expression twisted in a mix of fear and something else I didn't quite understand. He licked at the blood on his lip, reaching for me again.

It was Merc who caught his arm and pushed it back. Then I knew. Betrayal. Cam took a step back and turned hard. "The fuck?"

"There's another way." I ground out to Preacher. "Right? Another way that he gets to walk?"

Preacher, realization brightening his eyes, waggled his bushy eyebrows. "Well, darlin', there just so happens to be."

Cam's shout was feral, angry, and echoed off the side of the building. Puck and Jester grabbed him as he dove for me again, and held him back.

Merc wouldn't even look at them, couldn't, because of what we were about to do. I closed my eyes tight as Preacher laughed. "I'll need a vote."

"Fuck no!" Cam struggled, tearing at Puck's arms around his, kicking at Jester as he stood in front of him, leaning on him, and pushing them all back.

"Yay." Merc said, then turned to Cam. "Her choice, brother. I can't let you do this."

When he looked at his father, something passed in that look that nobody else would understand.

AP, completely trusting his son, nodded his head and gripped Dekes on the shoulder. "Yay."

"The fuck?" Cam jerked again. "Are you fucking kidding me?" Puck gripped harder.

Dekes swore and looked away. "Yay."

The guy who had tried to intercept me and Drop Top, also yay'd. Jester, a yay which earned a buckling kick to the leg from Cam. Grimacing, Jester recovered quickly and held fast. I couldn't figure out if they trusted AP that much, or didn't like the idea of hurting Cam. Maybe a good bit of both.

"No. Nay. Fuck no." From Cam.

"Also, no." Puck grunted, still holding him.

I stopped looking at Cam and slowly lowered the pistol, which Merc took and slid into his belt. "I won't ride with you."

Never.

"Take your choice, gotta have witnesses, anyway." He sneered.

"I'll ride with Merc. And neutral ground—Ro's house?"

She wasn't there, which was the entire damn point. With a jerk of his head in agreement, Preacher turned and exited through the clubhouse. Drop Top and several others I didn't know followed him.

I kept my face from Cam, I couldn't look at him, and see that anguish again, knowing I put it there.

Merc took my hand as we went back the way we came. The louder Cam shouted, the angrier and more desperate his voice, the tighter Merc squeezed.

While I climbed on the back of his bike, he stalked to Cam's and shoved a knife into the back tire, then the front tire, each one popping with an angry hiss. "Buying us a little time or he'll be right on our ass."

But nobody would keep him from me that long. I'd seen the wild look in his blue eyes. I was counting on it.

I swore I could still hear him screaming as Merc tore out of the parking lot behind Preacher and the other guys.

Thirty-Three

CAM

She'd been glorious, beautiful, and beyond comprehension when she'd pulled Archer's forty-five. The sun made the red in her hair glitter as fiercely as the look on her face. I'd take all the pain, all the torture, for her.

And then my worst nightmare had come true. She was leaving, even as I shouted her name so loud I felt the blood vessels burst in my throat, as I threw my body against Puck's arms, dragging him through the grass. I fought with everything I had, but Jester was there, too. Maybe someone else. Full-grown men pulled me to the ground, holding me back to keep me from killing them all.

Because I would. Even Merc. The anger, the hate, the betrayal that surged through me jerked the bodies that held me forward.

My best friend disappeared with my girlfriend as I fought against Puck's arms. After the third or fourth solid kick landed against Jester's legs I put him on the ground with a grunt, he let go.

I only had Puck to wrestle with as the sound of Harley engines disappeared into the distance. My voice was so hoarse now, the screams were more croaks. What Preacher had done to Ro was unforgivable. But what he'd do to Riley—to hurt me? This wasn't just about fucking her to get back at me.

He'd break her.

My chest imploded. The pain-coated shards ricocheted inside me, even blinding me. None of them were my brothers, none of them were the people I'd pledged my loyalty to. When Archer died, he'd taken with him the parts of this club that made it special.

But he'd given me something more. A reason to live, a reason to fight, and while there was breath in me, I'd do just that—for Riley.

Cold, steel resolve gripped my muscles tight for an instant, then I gave up the fight and sank to my knees. My chest was heavy as the air burned my lungs with each breath, and a cold sweat made my skin clammy. The cotton t-shirt that clung to my skin was flecked with blood, and my hair fell into my face.

I was the perfect picture of a broken man...until Puck let go.

I shot to my feet, around the building, and to my bike.

"Mother fucker." It sat on two flat tires. Something sick sank in my gut.

"Damn." Puck skidded to a stop behind me before turning back to his bike.

Then I remembered Archer's bike, the key suddenly hot in my pocket.

"The bay door, Puck. Open the fucking bay door." I dashed through the front entrance of the clubhouse, slamming into Ivan and sending him tumbling into several others. He was shouting something, but I no longer listened. I threw a leg over and turned on the ignition. The old school kick-start was something Archer loved. And as I cycled through a few priming kicks, I wished like hell he hadn't.

Metal rattled as the engine roared to life on a final kick, and sunlight streamed into the clubhouse.

Other bikes were firing, too. AP, Jester, they all filed in behind me as from the clubhouse.

Ro's place. Riley. Not for the first time did I ride like hell for my girl. But this time, the desperation chased away all other thoughts. I'd break every finger on his hand if he touched her. I'd kill Merc for going with this, for agreeing to it.

Of all people, he should know how much she meant to me. He knew me the most.

I licked my lip. The metallic taste of dried blood waking whatever it was inside me I'd fought so hard to keep quiet. The violent mass of emotion that had killed a man would kill more today.

Riley hadn't calmed that beast. It lived. For her.

A glance in the rear-view mirror showed that I wasn't alone, not by a long shot. Everyone had followed, making up two rows behind me very similar to how I'd ridden Archer's bike the last time. Thinking about how Riley wasn't against my back, I ripped the throttle tighter, my t-shirt whipping around my middle.

I turned into Ro's place, searching for Riley. She stood in the driveway, not far from Merc's bike, beside the man I'd once thought was my best friend. But Preacher sauntered to her, swinging his arms like he was the biggest dick on the block.

He wasn't.

I don't know if I cut the bike off. I barely registered slamming the kickstand down with my foot.

"Preach!" I ran the instant both feet hit the gravel. I'd be damned if someone stopped me. I was more than three decades younger than him and faster. He'd barely turned when my fist struck his jaw, bone crunching beneath knuckles.

He stumbled back, my left punch drove him to the ground. I landed on top of him, swinging both arms. Short, rapid blows to his face. For Archer. For every snide comment. For destroying my club. For Riley. Skin split at my knuckles, across his nose. Blood poured from his face. A lone gunshot rang out.

I glanced up to see Merc standing over me, facing away, a nine-millimeter pistol raised. Hand fisted in Preacher's shirt, other one raised to deliver more punishment, I glanced over my shoulder.

Paul was on the ground, blood pouring from a bullet wound in the middle of his forehead and a gun in the dirt beside him. He'd been about to shoot me in the back.

All around us, Desert Kings stopped their forward motion and gawked at the scene in front of them.

Merc turned his pistol to another one of Preacher's cronies, as the man himself moaned and twisted beneath me.

"You're dead, kid," he breathed. I turned long enough to spit in his bloody face.

"One. More. Step." Merc ground out at the other guy, who put his hands up, palms out.

Ro's driveway around us was blood soaked.

"Cam." A warm, feminine hand rested on my shoulder.

I looked up to see Riley peering down on me. I'd expected fear, but what stared down at me was guilt, remorse even. With a hard shove, I pushed and stood, wrapping her in my arms to inhale the scent of her hair.

"I'm sorry." She looked up, forcing me to look at her. "But trust us just a minute longer."

She pulled away from me, leaving me staring at her as she walked to the lone blacked-out sedan in the driveway. For the first time, I recognized Ky Soletsky's car. Riley bent in the window, speaking earnestly.

Merc, his pistol still trained on Preach's man, was speaking to his father, and the others as bikes continued to roll into Ro's driveway and tidy front yard. As Ky rounded , pieces began to click into place.

I didn't trust many people. Merc and Riley were it. My best friend glanced over his shoulder. "Brother, Archer's forty-five is in my waistband. I'd feel a lot better if you had it until your finishes what she's started."

Preacher rolled to his knees, wobbled from side to side, and pulled his own from his vest. I kicked it away, as I gripped Archer's and pointed it at him. Fitting that I would kill him with Archer's gun.

Thirty-Four

Riley

Cam stood like a damn warrior, bloodied and beaten but strong. My dad's gun fit solidly in his long-fingered hand. I felt better knowing it was pointed squarely at Preacher, not Merc. I'd hoped what I'd done to that friendship could be repaired.

But if not, I'd done it to save Cam and would do it all over again.

Ky Soletsky was tall with golden hair and a mischievous smile even in the middle of a viper's den. Yuri was here too, standing guard at the back bumper. Sasha stepped from the car, fear causing her to move with quick, jerky motions.

"It's okay." I reminded her, taking her hand and leading her toward where AP and Dekes stood, several feet away from Merc and Cam—guns still drawn.

"I don't know anything about your rules," I started, surprised, when Sasha squeezed my hand. "But I have something to say."

I glanced back at Preacher, who wiped blood from his nose and glowered at me through a swollen eye. I should be angry, but Cam felt enough of that for both of us. I felt sick, cold, and hollow. He would die today, though I didn't want the club to bear that burden. None of them.

"My father didn't kill himself. Preacher killed him."

There were swears, shouts, and I was betting half of them didn't believe me. Then someone else took my free hand and brought it to his lips. I didn't have to look to know Cam was there, standing with me.

Jester, Drop Top, and Puck flanked Dekes and AP. The table, listening to what Archer's daughter and a Russian hooker had to say. It should be , or strange, but our entire future hung on this moment.

"It's okay, Sasha, you're safe here," Ky prodded from behind us with a gentle whisper.

AP nodded his agreement. Gone was the soft, fatherly expression he usually wore. He brooded now, much like his son, a violence awakened just under the surface.

She opened her mouth and shot her frantic eyes over to me. The uncertainty evident in the cold fingers that clutched mine. To her, these were the leather clad men of nightmares. Especially after what she'd experienced.

I started for her. "Sasha was with Archer the night he died at the motel. When his killer showed up, she and waited until he was long gone before she came out and called it in."

"Your uncles know this?" AP looked right at Ky, ignoring her completely.

"One did. And you'll understand why he kept his peace..." Ky gestured toward me.

"Sasha," I asked gently, "who did you see out the peephole that night?"

"Lying whore," Preacher spat from the ground beside me. When Cam moved toward him, I gripped him tight to my side. But Merc slapped him with such force the old man staggered on his knees.

"Sasha?" I asked again.

She pointed to Preacher. "It was that man."

"You sure?" AP asked.

"I saw him through the door and recognized his voice. They argued about money while I hid in the bathroom. Then he shot him. I waited until I heard him ride away. But when I came out..." She choked on a sob as I clung to her hand. "He was, he was gone."

"And you're just now telling us, why?" Dekes asked without any sort of aggression, and Preacher mumbled arguments at the rest of the guys who watched.

"What would happen to a whore who accused the president of the Desert Kings of murder?" She was more confident with each word. "It would cause war with the men I owe my life to."

Not looking at the body in the dirt near Merc, I searched the crowd. Those who'd rushed to Preacher's side were angling in a different direction now. Even Kenna's ex, Ghost, was moving closer to Dekes and AP.

A tall, bald biker from a different charter took Merc's place. It was only then I realized he was no longer fending off the rest of the club and had his pistol trained on Preacher.

Cam left my side as he, Merc, and the rest of the table stood in a small circle. Ky led Sasha back to the car, shutting the door and leaning against it to watch the show with Yuri.

"You've created quite the scene," he said, sounding amused.

"Yeah, well, I think it had to happen." Nervous, I rubbed my hands together.

Cam had shoved the pistol in his waist and watched me over AP's shoulder. I'm sure he listened, but the way he studied me was soothing. I was safe, even from this distance, so long as he was there.

I'd never forget the way he flew into Preacher, the violent way he'd hit him. He'd held that anger for as long as he'd known me. It had hidden inside, while on the outside he'd been my everything. I owed him for that. I only hoped this would be enough.

"What do you think they're saying?" Ky asked, pulling a bag of candy from his pocket and shaking out a few pieces.

The other guys milled around their bikes now, less confused and more shocked, as they waited on the table to decide Preacher's fate.

My heart beat a nervous rhythm until I saw Drop Top break off. His short, rigid as he spat in the dirt and stormed off to his bike, hopping on and peeling out of the driveway. A handful of guys followed him.

"Stand up," AP said to Preacher.

The big man obeyed, his body trembling—not with fear, but with hate. Every part of him looked past AP to Cam. AP ripped the president patch from Preacher's cut, pocketed it, then said something so low I couldn't hear it.

Whatever it was made the beefy man even angrier. He sputtered, blood and spittle hanging from his handlebar mustache.

"You little, lying piece of shit," Preacher growled at Cam.

"Nah." Cam shook his head. "I didn't murder my best friend because I have a gambling addiction. But that cash? It was right under your fucking nose."

Preacher spat in his face. Then dove for his gun as Cam stumbled, wiping the blood from his eyes. But he didn't point it at Cam. No, that wouldn't cause the pain he wanted. He knew he was going to die.

He was going to kill me first.

There was a moment of stillness where I accepted my fate. That this man, his face all busted from the hands of the man I loved, would kill me just as he had my father. But worse, Cam would watch him do it.

One shot. Two. Three echoed across the desert as I squeezed my eyes shut, waiting on the pain. Then five more in rapid succession, so loud that my ears felt like they might explode.

When no pain came, I opened my eyes. Cam stood arm out, Archer's chrome pistol shining in the rays of sunshine that broke through over the horizon.

The big man's body lay crumpled on the ground.

I was alive.

He wasn't.

Gravel crunched under my feet as I ran to Cam, throwing my arms around his middle and holding on with everything I had. Around us there was a flurry of activity, Ky and his crew leaving, some of the Kings as well. Funny how surrounded by gangsters I hadn't been scared at all. But now, my body gave and my stomach pitched. Had Cam not held me upright, I would have crumbled to the ground.

It was over.

Then he sighed once, heavy and laden with all the emotions of the day. "You come up with all of this?"

"This morning, yeah," I mumbled against him, not caring that his shirt was caked with dried blood and dirt, or that he'd just killed a man.

"Jesus. What could you have done if I gave you a week?"

"You don't want to know." Merc snorted.

I didn't need to look up to know Cam was glaring at him. He'd gone rigid, his body hard. "You owe me." Cam's voice was low, scratchy from the shouting and screaming.

"I know." Merc turned back to his father.

I looked then, watching AP issue orders. Some guys left to perform some sort of duty. The rest hovered around the two bodies.

I didn't look, didn't need to. Preacher couldn't hurt us anymore.

"Come on." Cam took my hand and led me toward my dad's bike. I watched as he threw his leg over and kicked down on the old school kick-start. He was gesturing me onto the back, when AP waved him over. Cam rolled across the driveway and pulled to a stop in front of the old man.

"There's a cut on the table in the chapel. Go put it on, son."

Cam closed his eyes, turned his face up toward the sky, and grinned. "You sure about that?"

"With every fiber of my damn being. Never should have taken it off." AP extended his hand.

Cam shook it, pulling him into a hug. There was brotherhood here, something Preacher had always been on the outside of...because he'd never understood the Desert Kings were about more than one man.

It was all of them.

I couldn't take Cam from that, wouldn't.

"Let's go home," I shouted, hugging him around his middle.

AP patted my shoulder as Cam turned the bike and rocketed down the driveway, putting distance between us and what had happened.

For the first time since my mom got sick, I was hopeful about the future. For my life. I had Cam.

Epilogue

Riley

I'm not sure what happened to the bodies, I just know that Cam took me home. We slept in his apartment, and for the first time he slept well into the next day, his body relaxed, his breaths even.

The next morning he went to the clubhouse, I guess to get their stories straight. I didn't ask questions, I knew everything I needed to know. Preacher had killed my father for the money. Cam had killed him. Cam Savage was in love with me.

Neither of us had to run anywhere. I knew who I was, who he was, and who I wanted us to be. This life my mom had been so afraid of, was one I'd been made for. Part of me was glad she wasn't here to know I was more like Archer than I was her.

As hard as Cam would protect me, I would protect him. Starting with law school, in Vegas, so we could split our time here at home. While he was gone, I had a lot of time to think. I showered, got ready, and was halfway to my car by the time he texted me to come to the clubhouse.

When I first pulled in, only a few familiar bikes sat in the gravel lot. But more pulled in behind me. Inside, Dylan was already behind the bar, flipping through a magazine. I went to her first, around the bar, to hug her tight.

"Thank you." She whispered against my ear, the emotion so thick in her voice that tears stung my eyes.

"They're my family too."

"Yeah, *we* are." She pulled free of me and gave me a smile. "My brother and Cam are on the roof."

I nodded and left her to her magazine, stopping long enough for AP to ruffle my hair at the bottom of the steps. He didn't say anything, didn't need to, his proud smile said it all.

On the roof, Cam and Merc stood at the ledge, looking out over the desert below them. The sun was setting, very similar to the first time Cam had brought me up here. Minus the big party and the bottle of tequila I wished I'd snatched at the bar.

Merc turned first, smiled but it didn't quite meet his eyes. "He's still pissed at me." We'd all been through so much in the past forty-eight hours. He looked tired and I felt that too.

Cam snorted, socked him in the shoulder, then turned and crossed the roof to me. He picked me up in a big hug, then kissed me until I couldn't breathe. "Hi." His eyes were red and he tasted of tobacco and maybe a little weed. I wouldn't doubt it.

"Y'all get it worked out?"

He shrugged. "Nothing to work out. Is there?" But something still hung heavy.

"I had no other choice. We needed them all to follow you."

"You worked it all out?" He tapped a finger to my temple.

"Yeah, I did. And I'd do it again." I looked past him to Merc. "You said he'd take care of me, he did. You aren't the only man to kill for me now."

Then the smile slid slow, the corners of his mouth turning up and his blue eyes sparkling. "Yeah, I kind of owe him now."

Merc's laugh was light. "I'm going to hold you to that."

"I love you." I snuggled against Cam's chest and he tightened his arms around me.

"I know." He laughed when I faked a knee to his groin. "I love you too."

The door slammed against the wall behind us.

"It's a great night for a party!" Jester's familiar, jovial shout made me chuckle. "For the lady." He bowed a little and handed me a half full bottle of tequila.

Puck was with him, hair pulled back, grinning. They all were, everyone was lighter—happier. Cam had slayed their dragon.

When Jester jerked Cam into a hug, I let him pull him from me, and opened my bottle. I took a swig as I sat in my father's chair on the roof. Puck sat beside me and tapped a beer bottle against my tequila.

"To Archer."

"Cheers to that." And I could say it. I hadn't known my father, but he'd given me the life I hadn't realized I needed. As much as Cam had, he'd saved me too.

"Kenna here?" It seemed a natural thing to ask Puck, since she was with him a lot—kept his kid.

"Nah." He shook his head, contemplated the bottle, but never took a swig. "I haven't seen her since…"

He let that trail off, but I knew what he meant. I'd only seen her the once, hadn't had a chance to see her more.

"No babysitting?"

"Nope." There were shadows on his face when he said it.

"She went through a lot, she'll come around."

It was his silence that hurt my heart. He may not say it, may not even know it, but what he felt for her was more than just a friend. I'd seen that in the tender way he'd carried her from that frat house.

Never one to let anyone brood for long, Jester shouted something at Puck that had the big man saluting me with his bottle and taking off toward the group of them. Cam peeled away and came over, taking his seat.

"You look serene." He turned and inspected me, before taking my free hand and twining his fingers with mine.

"And you look happy." I responded as he pulled my fingers to his lips and kissed them.

"I am. I wouldn't be here, without you." The matter-of-fact way he said it made me duck my head.

"Neither would I."

We didn't say anything then, just watched the sunset over the of his best friends, his family.

My family.

Sexy Little Brat and Daddy Issues Coming Spring 2025

To be the first to get copies and for exclusive excerpts before anyone else Join The Candy Shop on Facebook and sign up for my Newsletter.

Also By

Desert Kings MC
Book One: *Savage Lust*

More From Candi Scott *Fashionista's Playbook*

ABOUT THE AUTHOR

Candi Scott is the nom de plume of award winning author Leslie Scott. She has been writing stories for as long as she can remember. From kissing books to biker demi-demons and swamp witches she lives vicariously through each and every character. When not writing she lives and writes amidst her own happily ever after with her not so charming prince where they flirt relentlessly like twelve-year-olds and embarrass her teenage son. There's also domestic zoo wrangling, homeschooling, and animal rescue organization volunteering.

Find out more at Candi's Website

Printed in Great Britain
by Amazon

55318374R00138